FICTION

CYPRESS IN MOONLIGHT
  By Agnes Mure Mackenzie

SMALL TOWN
  By Bradda Field

FRIENDS AND RELATIONS
  By Elizabeth Bowen

STARDUST : A TALE OF THE CIRCUS
  By D. L. Murray

SO WE'LL GO NO MORE
  By Evelyn Pember

SHIP WITHOUT SAILS
  By B. Barclay Carter

IMPERIAL TREASURE
  By Val Gielgud

JUDAS AND OTHER STORIES
  By John Metcalfe

EARLY CLOSING

BY

D. WYNNE-WILLSON

CONSTABLE & CO LTD
LONDON

PUBLISHED BY

Constable & Company Limited
London W.C. 2

·

BOMBAY
CALCUTTA   MADRAS

Oxford University
Press

·

TORONTO

The Macmillan Company
of Canada, Limited

First Published September, 1931
Reprinted -   - September, 1931
Reprinted -   - October, 1931

Made and Printed in Great Britain by Wyman & Sons Ltd.
London, Reading and Fakenham

DEDICATION

To E.

PART I

MICHAELMAS

CHAPTER I

" . . . There is a harmony
    In Autumn, and a lustre in its sky,
Which through the Summer is not heard or seen."
                                        —SHELLEY.

ONCE upon a time there was a housemaster
    called William, who feared God, mistrusted
the Government, and moulded other men's sons
to the best of his ability.

On a silent morning in September he sat in the
sun at his breakfast table, and his thoughts boiled
together in a rich confusion.

He summoned his forces for the coming year.

He would do thus and thus, stamping out discord
amongst the servants and hooliganism amongst the
boys.

He would take a high tone with the matron, and
begin as he meant to go on with the new under-
housemaster.

Ailments should be kept in check, and
his own children acquire clean hands and soft
voices.

Cook-and-gardener wrangles must be subdued, as
also that calling down the backstairs.

Again in the Dining-hall he would have the piano

tuned, and in the Changing-rooms prohibit sponge-football and the gargling of the National Anthem.

Furthermore, prefects must cane in their studies and not on the landings, causing crowds to collect.

And in the wider sphere of the school itself he would curb his tongue, and not until the ripe moment lose temper in Common Room.

Thus garlanded with resolutions, he stared away over the lawns to where the gardener, so lackadaisical, was brushing away the worm-casts and disturbing the dew.

The letters addressed to W. Dean, Esq., arrived, and William opened them.

His letters came from parents, heralding the arrival of their offspring on the morrow. These letters, few, and invariably couched in the same terms, came as regularly as his assessment papers from the Inland Revenue ; had done since he took over the house six years ago, and would do so until he gave it up nine years hence.

William skimmed through them one and all, dispassionately. He looked upon their authors as one of the curses of the State.

One day he would write a letter to the Press about them ! Some there were who wrote hoping that their boy would be appreciated ; and others, fearing that theirs had not been understood.

Those few who had not discovered the artistic temperament in their sons, had found them to be highly strung ; and one and all would have him know that theirs was not the sort of boy to settle down easily into the rough-and-tumble of Public School life.

And William tried, as always, to forget the signatures, that the imbecilities of the parents might not be too heavily visited upon the children.

He cast aside his correspondence and held out his cup for more coffee.

" Ah ! " he said acidly, " a pretty handicap are parents to a boy at school ! " The orphan was indeed twice-blest.

He ran on a little in this vein, and Julia Dean did not interrupt her husband, knowing that he enjoyed his facetious grumblings. Had he not thrived on them for years ? So she sat still and deep in thought until there were brisk steps in the passage outside and, with a sharp twist of the door-handle, Miss Mary Greig was in their midst.

She had a large fat calf and high heel like the map of Italy. The approach of middle age had crystallised the ginger of her hair ; but she was well dressed and kept within sight of the fashions ; was up in current affairs ; kept an eye on the political antics of her own and other lands ; knew what books had been lately published or suppressed ; what plays were on ; what bishops had been appointed ; and who had lately died.

She had brothers. One was in oil in Mexico, so she knew what was happening in those parts. Another brother was in clover, so to speak, as an estate agent twenty miles away, and that was why she had come to this place. She fulfilled her matron's duties irreproachably throughout the day, and would of an evening play an excellent hand of Bridge, and never stung her partner by word or glance.

William rose up as she came brightly in, and cocking a sad eye gave her good morning, and asked if he might get her porridge, or whether she would go straight to fish or eggs ?

But she, with bird-like glance at clock and thanking him, replied that she had had breakfast a long, long time ago, and had only looked in to see if he could do anything about a pipe that was leaking in the airing-room.

But Dean said that he was only a Master of Arts, and that plumbing was out of his sphere. However, Kedge should look at it, but he did not fancy that would do much good !

Miss Greig, behind her perennial smile, regretted that Mr. Dean was never definitely gay or sad. All this melancholy jesting was so apt to warp the boys.

And the melancholy jester found her as irritating as ever. Invariably she jarred, save when she sang (as always) at House Suppers in a deep contralto. It was a pity she could not always sing. But although the world might be a stage, it could not of course be opera.

Mary Greig turned to Mrs. Dean and asked whether the car was going down to the village during the morning ; and if so, might she go too ? or would it suit better in the afternoon, when Mr. Fenn's train was to be met ?

Mr. Fenn was the under-housemaster, new this term.

Julia rose, stretched, and smiled at her, saying
that it made no difference.

Julia was slim and straightly made, and as tall
as her husband.   Between the matron and herself
was a peaceful understanding.

She never thought one way or another of her
own or other people's failings ; while Miss Greig
considered that even if Mrs. Dean did divide her
time between her golf and her music, it was no
concern of hers.   Everybody had a right to fresh
air, and as for the piano-playing, well, it was abun-
dantly clear to Miss G. that Mrs. Dean could have
made a very much better job of her music (giving
recitals, as she had done before her marriage) than
her husband was making of schoolmastering.   She
might be unpractical, but then the artistic temperament accounted for so much.   Unlike William, she
had not been brought up to believe it a mere
synonym for idleness.

But, however, she was not here to fritter away
her time in a sunny dining-room.

Turning briskly round upon her employer, she
said that as she was anyway going through the hall,
she could save him the trouble of going right down
there to put up the House Lists, by taking them
herself.

" No," said William, disapproving this circum-
locution, and answering her unspoken question—
" No, I have not yet written them out.   There are
no great changes, as Penhurst is having another
year ; except that Gray and Bentley are to be
House-Prefects."   At the mention of these last two

names Julia laughed outright, and Mary Greig pursed up her lips and then said something generous about old poachers and gamekeepers, a phrase so often on the estate-agent's lips, and pertinent in this case, she hoped.

She tried to think charitably of Oliver Gray and could not. It was just a year and a term since he (tired of wet weather and work overdue and unattempted) had smacked himself heavily upon the chest with a hairbrush, and come to her. And she, with one look at his chest, had clapped him into the sick-room—a case of German measles; here, after some five hours' siesta, he had been unmasked by William and the school doctor, and beaten. But the tale had gone about. "You may well smile," said William to his wife, "at this choice of two flippant scallywags. But the Headmaster wishes them to be steadied by responsibility. I pray they may be." And he went on to say that things had come to a pretty pass if prefectships were to be used merely as a check on the downhill rush of the unsatisfactory. "And those two don't even mean well."

"Bentley has a younger brother coming this term, has he not?" And Mary Greig hoped he would be steadier altogether.

"And what of the other boys?" she asked.

William spread his hand towards the surrounding litter of correspondence. He began to pick and delve amongst it. Presently he uncrumpled something and said: "' . . . My husband and I feel sure that you will like him . . .'—Why?" William

asked the ladies from the depth of his heart ;
" . . . yes, and he shaves twice a week already,
as she tells me with pardonable pride. Well, well,
we shall see what we shall see."

And William passed through the French windows
into the garden. Out there his mock irritation
left him. Now he was a mellow pessimist
steeped in an Elizabethan melancholy ; but as
he lit his pipe a deep contentment surged in
upon him.

Perhaps it was the golden stillness of the morning, or the mushrooms for breakfast. The flowers
were still, and hung heavy with the dew ; a velvet
bloom upon everything. A bird called clearly, and
one flew near him with a taut flutter of wings.
And bees passed him humming in the warmth.
At the bottom of the garden he went through a
door set in a wall, and came on a cricket field, a
secluded spot usually set aside for the use of elderly
duds, that they might enjoy the National Game
in unskilled privacy.

Beyond this lay his juniors' football field, and
beyond this again the ground dropped away with
sloping fields and beech woods to the village, set
about by marshes and lying on the floor of a wide
and shallow valley.

William walked across the field. The turf was
spun with gossamers, long shining trails caught by
the sun.

Yet the light did not seem to come from the
sun, but to be around him in the air. And there
was mingled with the warmth an autumnal

sharpness ; a coolness ; a heady tingle, as if the air came from a snowfield.   Below in the valley there was haze, and the blues deepened between the trees.

The land was blessed in an autumnal peace ; a perfect fulfilment of the summer.

*　　*　　*　　*　　*

At the far side of the field was a cinder-path running between lime trees, and William went down it towards the kitchen gardens.   Presently he came upon Kedge, the gardener, prodding a bonfire.

He, when he saw his master, touched his cap, slid it back on his head and wiped the unexplainable sweat from his brow—all in a unique gesture—and then paused for rest and conversation.

But William stood gazing up the garden.   In the stillness the smoke went up straightly from the fire taking all colour from the trees beyond.   He sniffed and the smoke stung his nostrils.

" When you've done with this, Kedge, you might go and have a look at one of the airing-room pipes. It's leaking.   Miss Greig will tell you all about it. Leave it unless it's a simple job.   I shouldn't think there's much wrong, though.   Perhaps you can get it done before lunch."

Kedge said with confidence that he'd see to it straight, and that a knock or two would settle it. William quivered.

" For mercy's sake be careful, my good man, and don't go lashing at it and raising fountains, will you now ? "

Kedge in meekness took back all he had said, and changed his weight on to the other foot.

William continued. "Mr. Fenn," he said, "is bringing his dog with him. I told him not to bring a kennel, as he might just as well use Bran's. But clean it out well, will you, and put the straw in right up to the roof. It soon squashes down."

Bran, a collie, had died the previous spring of acute rat-poisoning, and William did not like his children to grow up without a dog. At the moment they had a lot of odoriferous rabbits, which was very unsatisfactory.

"And what sort of a dawg will ut be, sir?" asked Kedge.

"A terrier, wire-haired, I think."

"Well, it'ull come in nice and handy for the ratting, then, and the ratting 'ull be the better for another dawg." He flung down more leaves upon the fire and the smoke rose thickly. "And it 'ull be lively to have a little dawg about the place again. So it will." He thought that over, and added that the place would be more lively with a little dawg.

William agreed abstractedly. Kedge's conversations always put him in mind of the Psalms, in that he rephrased and repeated each idea. Being a Primitive Methodist, however, it was unlikely that he was consciously aping their parallelism. And how was Kedge's parrot? Kedge's parrot lived in a potting-shed. It appeared that the bird was doing nicely, but that it was not keeping its colour.

"It was dyed, as like as not, when you bought

it," said William, who had no illusions as to commercial morality. And advising Kedge never to leave it about in the rain, he went off up the garden, past the pigsties and the potting sheds, and between two green-houses with chrysanthemums inside, their leaves pressed against the glass. Then he went down another path so narrow that dew-drenched cabbages almost touched across it, and his ankles were sprinkled most deliciously. The sun was bringing the smells out of the earth, and William found this wet warmth quite intoxicating. And working hand-in-hand with Nature, Kedge had produced on all sides a rich and tangled profusion.

William skirted a wall and, turning a corner, met the two gardeners' boys.

Cretinous, they were, with small eyes, wide mouths and close-shaven scalps. One day he was going to put them into blue smocks to complete their French peasant resemblance.

Opening a gate, he came into the orchard, heavy with apples, and there found his children and the turkeys; two turkeys strutting in the grass. Beaverbrook and Rothermere, he called them. The children, a little way off, waded in the long grass, with their backs to him, their heads bright in the sun, intent upon their own affairs.

Juliet was talking to her rabbit, damp and frightened in the grass. Peter, cleaning out a hutch, held a rake in one hand and his nose with the other. Andrew, William's firstborn, directed, his hands in his pockets and his jersey all plucked by brambles. All these had Julia's brown eyes and white, uneven teeth. Their hair, like William's, was fair and straight. Peter and Juliet had theirs cut by their mother as soon as it got into their eyes ; but Andrew went to the barber's in the village, where for sixpence they disclosed his scalp in patches.

He had the chronic bad manners and full-blooded insolence of the Infant Prodigy without its brains. He was difficult from morning till night ; but William said : " Wait till he is old enough to understand my sarcasms." This would not be for some time. He was eight now and his birthday came in December.

" In a quarter of an hour," he said, " I'm going down to the village, and those with partings and dry socks may come too. But finish turning out that hutch and make this poor creature comfortable. Meet me outside the Barn."

The Barn, where William stored his car, was all that remained of a farm, upon whose site his house now stood. This farm had been burnt down in the year of Waterloo, during patriotic revelry. But William never believed that the news could have percolated down to these parts at all, and certainly not in the same year as the battle. However, that was of no consequence ; he had his ample barn, which he allowed year by year to silt up with all manner of junk.

Unswept it was, and garnished with old doors and rotting window frames, ladders, sacking, planks and barrels, together with a lot of old furniture clustered round a dumb piano in a corner, and certain wedding presents with ten years' dust upon

them. There were also toboggans, a bath-chair
and a mailcart, to say nothing of the children's
superannuated perambulators; and William was
fond of saying that he had once caught sight of a
penny-farthing bicycle!

And now the car had edged its way in near the
door, and it was probable that this man Fenn would
in time have one too, and then the junk would have
to recede further into unprobed darkness. High in
the gloom by the rafters there were bats, and the
place had its own private smell.

It was out of bounds for the boys, nor were
parents shown over it. The roof had been de-
thatched in favour of pink tiles, in case of fire and
by order of the Governors, as the Barn was so close
to the house. And William often said that if he
hadn't had his wits about him, they'd have fobbed
him off with corrugated iron.

Miss Mary Greig had only once been inside the
Barn and that was with Kedge to fetch a step
ladder, after the one in the linen-room had broken
and let her down.

Nothing, not wild horses, should induce her to go
there again! She considered it disgraceful that a
man like Mr. Dean who made such a fetish of tidiness
in some directions, should have allowed his Barn to
assume such a discreditable appearance, cluttered
up with rubbish and dry-rot and worms at work on
that good furniture, simply falling to pieces in the
darkness. But William was one of those who have
a military worship for personal tidiness, and yet
thrive in disorderly surroundings. The sight of an

untied shoe-lace or a dog's ear flapping back inside
out, or even Nature's little untidinesses such as
projecting teeth, irritated him unspeakably, so he
said.   But the state of his own study and dressing-
room was such that few housemaids could be got
to go in and dust them.

William was proud of his study with its bay
windows overlooking the garden, its gracious length,
and parquet floor pale as honey.

On the walls hung his Oxford prints.   There was
one of the High Street in sun and shadow, with
the clouds rolling away overhead and a string of
Edwardian sandwichmen going past the Examination
Schools for ever.

Opposite were his father's college groups, quaint
and bewhiskered ;   and his own, with himself
strangely the same as now ;   fair-headed with
square shoulders, staring, with his unchanging
expression of perplexed hilarity.

When he looked at these mildewed photographs
he was struck, and said so, by the steadiness in the
young men's faces.   Not that they were particularly
steady ;   but they lacked, thank God, that fly-away
look of gutless sophistication he fancied he saw upon
the faces of certain of his nephews, their friends and
contemporaries.   Nor was that all, for William
latterly in Oxford had seen a young man with a
beard, and it twisted his vitals that such a thing
should stalk the streets unharmed, unflung into a
pond !

Over the mantelpiece was a portrait of his grandfather ;   a good one, for the eyes followed him all

over the room. But Julia said this was no test at all.

Above the college groups was a shelf of pewter beer mugs and some ironstone dishes that fell down from time to time, but never broke. There was besides a copper warming pan which caught the firelight cosily in winter.

All along the remaining wall were bookshelves built in, whilst William's mathematical textbooks were stowed away in a revolving book-case which he could twirl without leaving his chair by the fire.

In term-time the centre table was stacked with work to correct ; and his canes, along with a landing net, odd curtain poles and a foil, were thrust away out of sight behind the piano. As William returned over the field from his tour of the kitchen gardens, his house came into view between the trees, with its uneven roof and all the creepers turning crimson. The private house was L-shaped, while the boys' wing, running out behind, had been added later. The back of the boys' quarters faced the Barn, with an intervening courtyard, where William backed and turned fiercely about in his car. And lately a hose had been installed there to irrigate the vehicle and peel away the clustered mud from underneath its wings. Unhappily—most unhappily—the kitchen also gave on to this courtyard ; and what with the chronic arrival of tradesmen's van and cart, that, toiling up the hill from the village, fetched up there with a sweep—horses a-lather and radiators a-boil —the comings and goings of Kedge and his under-lings—the way the servants laughed as only servants can, and the cook's little trick of putting her head out of the window to tell them what she thought of them from the bottom of her heart—well, all this went to produce an atmosphere redolent of a tavern in Pickwickian times, rather than of the back premises of one of the more conspicuous, if not leading Houses of an English Public School. This state of affairs was in no way any fault of William's ; merely one of his heavier crosses. How could he help the position of his kitchen, or moderate the voices of its staff ?

Moreover, was not his predecessor along with the Headmaster, the Governors and the school architect, gravely at fault in building the new wing in that direction ? Now had it formed, with the private house, the third side of a square, instead of straggling out at the back, the boys would have been without the distractions of the courtyard, and well surveyed by the private house.

And William brooding on these things heard Julia playing in his study ; deep chords, full and measurely ; Brahms he thought ; and he turned away skirting the wall of his garden, and went in by the boys' entrance down a long corridor with study doors on either side, and into the dining hall at the far end of the wing.

Here he was at once oppressed by the holiday silence of the place. The floor had been lately scrubbed and the inkstains brought up clear and fresh for the coming term. Protruding nail-heads caught the light, polished by scraping feet. The walls of the dining-room were a dim red. Six years

25

ago when Dean had taken over the house, that same architect who was so gravely at fault, had proposed a white distemper to give light. But William had swept him aside saying he had no wish for the place to look a cross between a slaughter-house and a Baptist chapel. And that had put him in his place !

Remembering his face, William chuckled, and looking at his watch shot away through dark passages into the private house and out into the courtyard, where blinking in the light he precipitated himself behind his steering wheel, and drove away out of the gates and down the hill, with all the children in the back craning their necks like chickens in a crate.

CHAPTER II

" L'air vif, âpre, sentait je ne sais quoi d'inconnu ;
et un bruit . . . à la fois faible et immense se faisait
entendre derrière les petits montagnes de sable."
—P. Loti.

THAT night two hundred miles away, a boy
in William's House was bathing on a lonely
coast, a shelving coast with currents that swept
along it and out with the receding tide.

To-morrow he would return to school, and his
last year would be his brother's first. His name
was Nigel Bentley, and now at midnight he and his
brother Johnny came up out of the sea and lay on
the sand. The water swirled up to their feet and
fell away leaving a line of yellow surf, bright with
winking bubbles gleaming and iridescent in the
moonlight ; and they broke, leaving a foam, air-
lifted, and it melted vanishing. Johnny raised his
head. The long stretches of sand unscarred and
pale under the moon, set him longing to run in great
mad wide curves like a dog, *ventre à terre*. He
sprang up and dashed into the surf again. He stood
on his hands, wrist-deep ; and the returning water
sucked the sand from underneath his palms, and he
fell over, sprawling. He stood up and pushed his

27

hair into a crest. It was quaint reddish hair, that kept its colour under water like seaweed.

"Now swim, my good boy," said Nigel, coming up behind, and trundling him into deep water left him and swam away smoothly, the water silken against his skin ; and the summer's warmth lingered in the sea. Johnny followed afar off, splashing and spitting. He swam in a jerky breathless way, his chin high out of the water.

And suddenly the loneliness of the sea and of the coast came upon him, and the place appalled him. Voices, lighted windows and food were so far away now. He was swimming dead away from them, too—straight out to sea ; and there was no certain land between him and beyond the North Pole ; some God-forsaken spot in Russia, so they said. And supposing they were drowned, the two of them, with not even bathing dresses on, and washed up in their skins and laid out on mortuary slabs ! And the fact that he had no bathing dress on made him feel more lonely than ever, utterly cut off from civilisation.

In his panic he gasped and gulped and swallowed, sending the water up his nose. His legs were no longer functioning. They sank and struck sand immediately. In all he had not moved more than a yard towards the Pole. The clutching terror of the mortuary slab fell away and he walked proudly about on the bottom of the sea, the water level with his upper lip. He could breathe but not speak.

Nigel came racing in past him, his black head submerged and his arms flashing.

They dressed. Johnny climbed gratefully back into his trousers and blew his nose on his towel.

Reaching the low huddled forms of the sand hill, they looked back at the sea and heard it breaking relentlessly and hushed ; sucking on the shingle. Then farther out and suddenly, a long wave broke and sweeping in left a stretch of water, mottled with surf. The tide had turned. On the sand hills the grasses bent, sighing, for there is always a wind on that shore. Nigel said it was a pity they couldn't sleep out here.

" It's as warm as June, and yet there's a kick in the air," he said. " And the day after to-morrow we'll be playing Rugger, and I shall run myself into a frenzy and I shall throw a fit and there will be head-lines in the papers : ' Boy froths at mouth on footer field,' and up and down the land headmasters will be asked to give their views on ' Over-arduous Athletics in Autumnal Heat.' " He shook his head over this dismal chain of events. " And there won't be another night like this till next year," he added dropping his voice, for it seemed to boom amongst the dunes, disturbing the country-side for miles.

Once, upon an autumn night like this, William had caught him strolling upon the " duds' pitch " in pyjamas, the turf rough under his bare feet. And William when he had had his say, added in truculent pessimism, looking up at the sky wide and moonlit, that a night like this put man and his goings-on in their proper proportion to the universe.

William and his universe ! Grieving over it !
And Nigel caught up Johnny floundering in sand
and tweaked his hair that sprouted like a sweep's
brush from the crown of his head.

" Home ! My good boy," he said.

' My good boy ' came automatically as a result
of four years' contact with his housemaster, for
although William spoke disparagingly of the human
race as a whole, he addressed its members as ' my
good man, boy, friend, fool or madam,' as the case
might be.

By the car they came upon their sister Lavender
asleep. She lay with an upturned face, one hand
behind her head and the other palm upward on the
grass.

Johnny dropped on his knees beside her and
tried to open an eyelid without waking her ; a ploy
that in the nursery had been used to while away the
interval between the time of waking and the time
of getting up.

Nigel started the car, and in the noise she woke
and sat up with wide eyes.

" Wherever are we ? I thought I was at home
in bed ! "

Then she saw Johnny kneeling by her, and Nigel
by the car, whose engine at that moment petered
out, and in the hush she heard the sea beyond the
dunes.

" It must be after midnight," she said, and
stretching, got up to look at the clock in the car.
It was a quarter past twelve.

Moths came and went in the shafts thrown by

the headlights. They climbed, all three of them, into the front of the car, Nigel driving, and it crept forward rocking over the uneven ground, past a pond mantled with duckweed, and a windmill, and out through a gate on to the road.

Here they gathered speed, and Johnny snug between his brother and sister, a nice damp towel round his neck and sand between his toes, felt his skin tingle from the salt water.

They rushed inland, swallowing up the road in great gulps. Above, the wires dipped and swayed, seeming to run level with them, and their tyres made a humming suck upon the road.

Moths came against the windscreen, and once Nigel swerved to avoid a rabbit, dazed by their lights.

They passed through a village with chestnut trees standing dark and heavy in the moonlight. And there by a wall was the glitter of a cat's eyes. On they went and the wind swept the sleep from their eyes and tore through their hair. Nigel sang and whistled, drumming his fingers on the wheel. By and by he slowed down, for the road was up, and they crept past a watchman in a hut, drowsing over a brazier ; and their faces glowed as the rush of air relaxed.

Soon after they left the high road and, dropping downhill under trees, stopped on the crown of a bridge. It was a hog-backed bridge, and getting out of the car they leant over its parapet.

Below, the water gurgled on the stones.

" Do fish rise all night ? " asked Johnny.

No one replied. Johnny sniffed and stroked his nose. The tip was as chill as a puppy's; he stared down into the water below.

They knew every stone of this bridge. It was just three miles from home, and always in summer throughout their childhood they had come here in their prams or walking beside them with the dogs. On the bridge they would stop, to be lifted up and left a little while to hang there with in-turned toes, gripping the parapet between the upper arms and stomach, while the nurses gossiped and the dogs prowled and sniffed and scratching snapped ardently at flies.

Delicious moments, gazing down into the pool with its polished surface dimpled and ringed by gnats, and beyond the pool the water's flow that combed the dark green weeds. And to disturb that polished surface with a spit that set reflected features a-waggle as if in sudden mirth or ague!

Later they had come here with Mark in the evening to watch him waiting for the trout to rise and hold his landing-net.

Then the pools had been yellow from the sky and cows just sitting about, and you could hear gaffers grumbling two or three fields away, it was so still.

Since then the parapet had shrunk away until it was level with Nigel's knees.

And to-night the pool was shadowed by the bridge, and the stream winding, caught the moonlight.

As they neared the house they saw one lighted window, and that, said Lavender, would be papa

watching and waiting in a masked despair. It was.
Their father heard the car approaching with an
exquisite relief, and when they surged in upon him
he was sitting, a long, lean widower, toying with
the *Exchange and Mart*.

But they knew him and asked in their flippancy
if he had managed to refrain from ringing up the
mortuary or not ? And they clapped him on the
back and told him what sort of night it was outside,
and how warm the water had been, and how
Lavender had slept through it all, thinking she was
at home in bed, the ninny ! Mark lay back in his
chair with closed eyes, lulled by the din they
made.

Nigel tossed himself into a chair, his legs spreading
half across the room, and Johnny went off to find a
biscuit.

When he came back he sat down on the floor, and
leaning against Mark's chair tucked a spare biscuit
into the turn-up of his trousers, near to hand, and
eating, stared at his brother and sister in a detached
way he had, as though he were seeing them both
for the first time.

Mark removed the damp towel from his neck and
tweaking the sweep's brush said mournfully that
the child's ears should have been trained up against
his head when young and tender, and not allowed
to grow protruding so distressingly. But Johnny
said he did not wish them any different.

" You'll get them torn off playing Rugger," said
Lavender. " You must wear a scrum-cap. I
wonder how you'll get on to-morrow."

33   C

" Very nicely, probably," Johnny answered. He found her interest rather tedious. She seemed to be thinking far more about his departure than he was himself.

So he got up and went to bed, and loosening his garments on the way upstairs, slammed the door of his room, climbed straight into bed, pulled the legs of his pyjamas over his toes, wriggled himself into a ball, buried his nose in the pillow and slept.

The others stayed talking about a new master called John Fenn who would be coming to stay at Christmas because Mark had known his mother. Insufficient grounds for foisting her son upon us, thought Nigel. Has he no friends ? Then he too went to bed and hunted through a book of modern plays. He was looking for something chaste, witty, and suitable for a House-play.

Mark went round locking doors and then retired, disrobed, said his prayers, wound up his watch, and turned out the light.

Lavender sat by her window in the moonlight, grieving. She told herself that she could never be any more to her brothers than a facetious creature who met them and saw them off, and wrote them exaggerated accounts of trivial home-doings, and took an annoying interest in their affairs. Well, she would write shortly and very rarely this year, until she got to Paris, and then there would be something to say. And they left to-morrow, and she wasn't going to Paris until Easter.

She sat on, unhappy, and yet content in her self-pity.   Happy to be awake and smell the Autumn in the garden.

But Johnny slept and slept.   At two o'clock he was roused by the hellish squall of cats.   But that only made him feel the more secure.   His nose went deeper yet into the pillow and he slept again, dreamlessly, and woke at seven with the sun on his face.

CHAPTER III

" . . . it being the first day of the term, which
was the first time I ever saw any such solemnity."
—Pepys.

IN Common Room the Masters talked, as black as
crows in their gowns.

Augustin Throssell spoke clearer than they all.

For twenty-five years he had taught English
Literature to the Middle School in an atmosphere
of undisciplined benevolence alternating with out-
bursts of petulance.

Those hours spent in company with immature
minds were a brief purgatory easily forgotten, while
with the Sixth Form his sensitiveness vanished. He
was calm and spoke with a width of understanding
of England's poetry and her writers, together with
those of other lands ; for he was a linguist, and
spent the greater part of his holidays walking in
France, or at his brother's villa in the Euganean
Hills.

Throssell gave the impression of having great
immaterial possessions, and a peace of mind which
amazed his colleagues when they considered the
din that proceeded from his classroom. But he
lived on unscathed by the roaring indolence of

junior boys. The noise, the discomfort, and his vain hootings for silence, speedily vanished from his mind, a transitory side of life, no more connected with him than that brawling, garbage-and-hurdy-gurdy world he stumbled upon in the purlieus of the Blackfriars Road, when he lost his way to the Old Vic.

Throssell was a quaint, short-legged creature with a bald head, far-away eyes, a deep voice and turned-out toes.

He had a passionate love for the beauty of spoken English, and in Chapel read the Lessons in a way that took the fidgets out of the whole company. His colleagues' wives, when in rotatory discussion of every soul in the place, summed him up very quickly. He should have been a Don, they said. As it was he lived content, a close friend of the Headmaster, and his House thrived under his wife and a succession of strong prefects. That sympathy given him so liberally behind his back was superfluous.

On this first day of the scholastic year Throssell stood talking in the Common Room before Chapel, with William Dean, a particular friend of his ; and Warner, an historian of sound political and religious views. The fourth member of the group was one Clovis-Abel de Mesière, a Frenchman, who having obtained among other distinctions a " certificate of pedagogic aptitude," had come to this college in grey Albion to prove its worth.

He had common bonds with Augustin Throssell. One was that their respective nicknames galled them. De Mesière chafed under " Frog," an insult to himself and race ; whilst even the visionary and un-selfconscious Augustin was vexed at times in the knowledge that he was known to all and sundry as " Teacher." Just " Teacher," a terrible name ; suggestive of the eternal chant of multiplication tables in hygienic, red-brick buildings, surrounded by railings and barren gravel !

He supposed some chance word of his in the past had given birth to the name, and that the wag who had christened him had long since departed. He might have been killed in the War, or perhaps survived to settle down and marry and enter his sons for the school. When " Frog " had said : " Is not ' Teacher ' the name given by all students to their professors in America ? " he had found no comfort, replying grimly : " Wait until they discover your name's Clovis-Abel," and then the whole matter had slipped from his mind.

The other link between these two was the fact that Throssell could speak to Clovis-Abel in his maternal tongue without making him wince.

Julia Dean could, as well, but no one else.

But there was someone else, as yet undiscovered ; a fair young man sitting over by the door of the Common Room, watching Throssell and his friends.

This was John Fenn, William's new under-housemaster, who had said nothing to Clovis-Abel the night before at William's dinner party, content to listen and watch. He had been brought up in Paris, for his mother, Mark Bentley's friend, had a

flat there. Some time he would get to know
de Mesière, but last night there had been no time ;
it had been so strange and talkative with Mrs. Dean
asking for news of his school, where her brothers
had been, and the man Dean arguing with de Mesière
over some Russian they had seen playing Hamlet.
And besides de Mesière there had been an incredibly
cheerful lady called Greig, with whom Dean had
conversed in a fierce gloom that had in no way
diminished her optimism. After dinner Mrs. Dean
had played Chopin in Dean's study, and then they
had all gone suddenly to bed.

And now, this morning, here he sat in full fig,
" black-tasselled trencher " and all, waiting, time-
table in hand, for the Chapel bell to ring ; and
outside, the trees stood mist-shrouded in the quadrangle. The mists were moving, like thick honey,
and now and then the sun appeared, round and
dull, looking like the moon.

This room was less like a dentist's waiting-room
than he had been led to expect. It was spacious,
with open windows, and filled with men—fifty or
sixty, he should guess. And as he looked dis-
creetly about him Dean came up, his face all
crumpled in smiles. In the distance a bell began
to ring, and these Masters and Bachelors of Art
arose and departed in a body to pray.

The previous evening William had spoken to
Johnny ; and Johnny had found him invigorat-
ing.

Towards the end William said :

" Now nothing I say can force you to work.

But please, my good boy, don't work at all unless you do it with the whole of your intelligence; concentrated; and then if it's only for an hour a day it will be worth while. And if you *must* stare round the room in form, just see to it that you know all about the pictures on the walls; and when you gaze out of the window, please to notice whether it's an elm or a lime outside, and what bird is twittering on the branches. There are many sorts of idleness, and putting off getting to work is no worse than working slackly when you do begin. And if you copy people who are slack when they work, and idle away their leisure as well, you'll be tired out and fit for nothing. If there is no work, then there's no leisure either. And that's why the forecasts of Heaven in the hymns are so particularly distasteful; what with no labour, no sleep to bring rest from labour, golden crowns, glassy seas, no shade, and not a tree in sight! But still, you needn't worry your head about that." And then he had asked after his father and sent him away.

That had been last night, and William had seemed a stranger, but now this morning he had heard him addressing the House after breakfast. And this William was familiar. At last he had seen him; and it was startling to hear that voice which had proceeded incessantly in recent years from Nigel's lips, coming out of the man's own mouth.

Never, never, had he heard such grumblings! So brisk and passionate!

For in William's grumblings there was no whining complaint. He had long ago accepted the view of the man who held that life was ' short, brutish and nasty.'

Maybe there were people who in the fell clutch of circumstance—and he, as a schoolmaster, would include himself—had not winced nor cried aloud.

Well, nor did he wince. He merely continued to unpack his heart with words ; and it was this back-chat with Fate that carried him on from day to day, round the revolving year.

And to have him grumbling here at hand was in itself an insurance against the worst. For while he kept an eye on the darker clouds, his household would enjoy the silver linings.

Johnny pondered over him, as after dinner that first day of term he strolled out upon the cricket field, waiting for Nigel. William, he was sure, ought to have been a road-mender or an under-taker, or a chucker-out ; and then he would not have had to think so much.

There was no sign of Nigel, or of anyone for that matter, but he was not sorry to walk about alone after the morning, for his head was buzz-ing.

He had told Lavender that he would get on very nicely, and so he had ; inconspicuous in the turmoil. In the House, too, he had passed unnoticed as a younger brother with a familiar name. And he was to be Gray's fag. He knew Gray, who had been to stay with them, talking, as Nigel did, in

William's voice. He had not seen him yet because he was arriving a day late. Reaching the rougher turf of the football field, Johnny walked on beneath the huge white H's, shining in the sun. He came to the far side, overlooking the valley. He stood at gaze. Below, the stubble gleamed in the fields, and chickens pecked around the distant stacks.

John Fenn, also recovering from the morning, stood in the doorway of William's garden wall, smoking, and watched the small boy on the skyline. His terrier walked about his feet.

As he stood there a boy came out of the gate by the corner of William's wall, his hands deep in his pockets. He was very tall, with black hair and a wide mouth. Fenn had noticed him at prayers the night before. Then another boy came running through the gate.

He was of middle height and broad, with thick brown hair and a parting running steeply uphill. His high cheekbones gave him an air of permanent joviality.

The two of them stood within twenty yards of John Fenn, and shook hands up and down for some time.

" My good boy, what happened ? Why didn't you come yesterday ? "

The broad one opened his mouth, pointing. " A tooth," he said, " a very bad tooth. It came on suddenly. I had it out, a frightful wrench. Then I wired to William. And how is William ? " he asked with a sudden tender gravity, as if inquiring for a new-born child.

" As well as can be expected," replied the other in the same strain.

John Fenn's mouth twitched. Then he realised that conversations such as this were not for him. He retreated into William's garden, but his terrier trotted out on to the field beyond the trees and lay down in the sun.

" What is that ? " asked Gray, pointing at it.

" Ah ! That's William's understudy's dog, that is," said Nigel.

" Too high on his legs and too short in the muzzle. Puts me in mind of a lamb. What is this man Fenn like ? "

" Oh, he looks about a year older than us. I haven't spoken to him yet. I must though. His mother is a friend of my father's. He took a table at dinner. I saw him in the distance, eating up his gristle."

Gray said he liked a man to swallow down everything that was put before him. It was a good example to the younger boys. Then he looked up quizzically at Nigel's tie ; his new prefect's tie, and squinted down at his own.

" And to whom do we owe this preferment ? Not to William, I'll lay."

" Oh ! I don't know. It often comes over me that he may think more of us than we do of ourselves, which is as it should be." And they began to laugh, and Nigel stood, one leg twined round the other, his hands to his ribs, spluttering.

" I must go and see William," said Gray. " And here's his child," he added, as Andrew came through the door in the wall, " up to no good, up to no good," he muttered. " I thought as much. Leave that dog alone instantly, sir," he shouted, in a voice sufficiently like the child's father's to make the child jump ; for Andrew had hold of Fenn's terrier by the back legs.

" I wasn't hurtin' 'im," he said in surly tones.

Gray appeared unable to speak. Red in the face, he bridled and fumed.

" You'd answer me back, you would ? Just because you have irredeemable bandy lower limbs yourself, you feel at liberty to twist those of another creature which are straight in comparison ! Unworthy scion of a most deserving house ! Now cut away and tell your papa all I've said," and Gray eyed him with automatic distrust as a housemaster's child. He began to tell Nigel how he would bring up Andrew if he belonged to him. They turned towards the house.

" I'm looking for Johnny," said Nigel. " I told him to wait for me here, but he's nowhere about."

" How is your John ? "

" Oh, he's all right. He's your fag, you know ; I arranged it with Penhurst this morning."

Penhurst was Captain of the House.

" Well, he'll have his time filled. I've just seen my other one. Spineless little maggot ! Looks as though he'd crawled out of a cheese." Gray shook his head, and asked Nigel after the rest of the family. Nigel said they were doing well.

" Did your father send me any message ? " pursued Gray.

44

" No."

" Oh, didn't he take to me ?   When may I come and stay again ? "

" When you're asked."

" You're a most uncivil boy.   That's the second rebuff I've had since my arrival. First Polly and now you."   And he said it broke his faith in Human Nature.

" What's Polly done now ? " Nigel asked, for Gray was always sparring with Miss Greig.

" Done ?   Oh, general coldness, general coldness. She swept by me in a corridor.   You know," he said, beginning to giggle, " the very sight of me sets her thinking painfully about my synthetically-spotted chest. Yes.   That was a sorry time for her."

" Well, it didn't turn out very comfortably for you either, did it ? " said Nigel, who remembered how Gray had appeared during tea straight from the sick-room, fresh from William's hands, red and muttering, to take his tea gingerly, and turn his back on the laughter and questions.   " William is a most interfering man," said Gray, " raising the sick is clean outside his province ; and to come and raise 'em forcibly like that and beat 'em ! Why, I've not been so startled since I was snatched from my cot in an air-raid in 1916 ! Oh, the whole affair was in deplorable taste ! And now I must go and see him, most exotic man."

But he did not.   Instead, he followed Nigel into his study, and told him how he had met " Frog " in check tweeds hunting for his napkin ring in the dining-hall ; for Clovis-Abel was attached to William's house for certain meals.

" And how is my fr-riend Fr-r-og ? " asked Nigel, the R's rolling up out of his throat.

" Oh, he should have a care, that man. He's putting on weight hourly."

" How do you know it isn't just sportive muscle ? "

" Oh, no, it's dead weight. I've seen him bringing it all along at the last minute into Chapel. Well, I asked him if he'd had an enjoyable vacation, and he said, ' But, yes, he passed a ravishing two weeks making foot-courses in the environments of Dijon with Monsieur Throssell, and that the weather has made good,' etcetera ; and I dropped my jaw and asked him to translate, and he did so and said it was a pity I knew so little of his tongue ; and I said that I, in company with the bulk of my compatriots, was ashamed of my linguistic deficiencies ; and he was very cordial, and we parted with much bowing and scraping. I could talk by the hour to him."

" Well, you can't talk by the hour to me now," said Nigel, " we shall be late for games. You go and see William." And he shovelled him affectionately out of his study. Gray came back.

" Send Johnny to me before tea, if you find him," he said, and was gone at last.

So when Johnny came back after a peep into William's vegetable garden, they were gone ; but on the turf was a little dog, so lovely that it took his breath away. A white, rough-haired terrier, marked in ginger about the head in perfect symmetry, with ginger ears and between them an enchanting row of ginger curls. Johnny dropped down beside him. The terrier rolled over on to his back, his paws lolling drowsily above a fine arched chest, and dreamily, with big brown eyes, gazed up into the empyrean.

Then all in an instant he grew alert, twitched himself on to his lamb's legs and cantered away, to jump up, with singing whines, upon his master, who had come out through the door in the wall. Johnny followed, worshipping.

The man said : " Timmy, get down." But Timmy did not get down ; he continued to reach up with vainly-climbing paws, and a brief tail—a mere bunch of curls—went to-and-fro in its groove.

Fenn pushed away his paws and the terrier ran round in little circles, and finally sank to rest with his back legs stretched out behind him on the grass. Johnny found him quite intoxicating.

" Is he yours ? " he asked.

" Yes," said Fenn, looking down upon the pair of them.

Johnny pressed Tim's ear, disclosing the white of his other eye, and very roguish the terrier looked.

" Have you got dogs at home ? " asked Fenn.

" Oh, yes. But not like this," said Johnny, fondly sleeking the ginger head. " Ours are getting stodgy. A Cocker and a Cairn." He did not say, ' sir,' nor did Fenn miss it, but they were recalled to their surroundings by junior boys, already changed for games, who, surging through the gate into the field, passed a ball about amongst them, laughing and calling out as they snatched at each other's legs.

They made their way over to the field beyond, while Fenn who was to take the game, and Johnny who was down to play in it, dashed away to change, horrified, and Tim, after a startled pause, streaked into the crowd.

CHAPTER IV

" A cook they hadde. . . ."
—CHAUCER.

IT was Sunday morning in William's kitchen.
Mrs. Turvey his cook stood muttering over a
cauldron.

If she were saying " Double, double, toil and
trouble," the phrase was in keeping with her
appearance. But she was stirring nothing more
sinister than vegetable soup for William's household to eat at midday.

As this simmered, chopped carrots and onions
were thrown up convulsively and cabbage leaves
trembled.

Beyond, in the direction of the scullery and
pantry, came the whirr of a knife machine, the
distant crash and rattle of plates and dishes, voices,
and the quick, heavy footsteps of people carrying
things.

A maid came in with a scuttle of coal. At once
she seemed to be in Mrs. Turvey's way, who swept
about her path, talking violently. The maid put
down the coal by the range, and slipped away,
shutting out the noise from the scullery. Then
the plate-box was dropped with a crash on the

49   D

flags, and the door opened again to admit Kedge in Sabbath clothes, with a basket in which he said were the last of they French beans. The old woman snatched it from him, tossing her head, and made off to the larder with a lilting stagger, and Kedge departed to his cottage of gentility, half-way down the hill to the village.

On the hearth before the oven door, drowsing in the warmth of the stove, sat a sleek little cat of good mousing stock, and disturbed by the draughty swirl of Mrs. Turvey's skirts, she raised her head and gave the old woman a green-eyed stare. Then closing her eyes again, withdrew into an upright slumber. It was a mild and sullen day. The kitchen was intolerably hot and the air heavy with food. Mrs. Turvey, still muttering, fetched pepper and salt from the dresser and threw them into the soup.

At that instant Julia looked in, and staring with round eyes into the fog besought Mrs. Turvey to open a window.

The old woman raised her strange, rheumatic hands and sweeping across the kitchen opened a window all on top of one of Kedge's underlings, who sprang away stung into a dazed activity.

Mrs. Turvey clapped the window to again, and made off back to the stove.

She had a wild and crazy glance and the blazing eyes of a fanatic. Indeed, she was a throw-back to pre-Renaissance times with a sackcloth-and-ashes strain in her mutterings, together with a bleak ' vale of tears ' outlook on life.

But she was quite harmless and no more responsible for her looks than is a gargoyle. She lived apart. Her general intelligence had long ago petered out ; but her cooking remained. Her large-scale meals for the dining hall were no better and no worse than those of other Houses ; but the dishes she produced for William's private table were of an incredible subtlety. Her gravies rich and delicious, afloat with little triangles of pale brown toast, lingered in the mind, a hallowed memory. Mrs. Turvey had an ever-swelling and tenacious compassion for William, rising as he did, poor gentleman, so early in the morning, and in black ! For his gown was to her a sign of perpetual mourning, and her cooking a votive offering to him in his unhappy circumstances. And if the poor gentleman could not afford good sherry in his soups, well then he should have Canary instead. And William cried : " Who the root-ti-ti-toot does she think I am to have my food soused with sack ? Falstaff ? " But he would never have parted with her, with Miss Greig suggesting so often that he should

He had picked her up two years ago when the House had been in the grip of influenza, and her predecessor had thought it a fit time to give notice. And was she not a genuine antique ? There wasn't a cook to hold a candle to her in the place. Good cooking William considered to be a moral uplift ; and of what advantage to his colleagues were their faultless table appointments if their teeth rebounded from their steaks and their soups winked greasily with ' eyes ' ?

Now the old woman was entirely competent in her own line. Strange she might be, comic she certainly was ; but of what account was one more, thought William, in a community which already contained oddities such as poor Mary Greig, Kedge and his parrot and his underlings, and crazy loons like Gray and Bentley ? The whole assembly was a pantomime. And just how and why it should have collected to revolve round him, he asked himself rhetorically, morning, noon and night.

So Mrs. Turvey was left untrammelled. She never went beyond the kitchen premises ; she haunted them week in, week out, rocking about the sunk brick floors. And it was supposed that she must sleep down there, for she was never seen mounting to her room, which lay under the roof between the servants' dormitory and the attic where was the main cistern, enjoying a fine view over the tree tops to the main school buildings, and a distant view of the Chapel beyond.

Perhaps the old woman knew when the trees were in leaf and when they were bare. More probably not ; for the heat in the kitchen remained equable, and her sole indication of the season's changes was in the varying garden produce brought in by Simon Kedge. The only time she regularly left her post was on Sunday at midday, when she washed her aged hands, took a clean cap from a drawer in the dresser, and climbed groaning into a rusty black confection " freaked with jet " that went on over everything else and hung during the week on the same nail as the grocer's almanac ; and then she set off lilting across the courtyard, through the boot-room and down a corridor to the dining hall ; where she stood at the carving table in a malevolent-looking trance, ladling soup from a tureen the size of a hip-bath.

The House were proud of her, and new boys were told that she was William's aunt. And on this first Sunday of term, in the early afternoon as was her custom after dinner, Mrs. Turvey drew up her wheelback chair to the fire and consulted her prayer book. This was a Victorian one. She went through the service and prayed a little uncertainly for Albert and the Queen, and shook her head over them, sighing " Oh, dear, dearie, dear, God bless them and God bless me poor heart." And she moaned over them, dimly and uncomprehendingly, as she moaned over William and over her ancient younger brother, who had been a market gardener, and though beneath the sward these ten years, existed for her still with all his financial failings and his corns.

These beings alone stood out clearly, landmarks in the haze, the great shapeless unanalysed Worry that was her life.

Then she closed her prayer book, crossed her hands upon her lap, and was aware of nothing save the warmth from the stove and its murmur, and the feel of her silk skirt against her fingers. . . .

The House was silent. The maids were upstairs, dressing to go out. William was in his study submerged in a Life of Disraeli; and John Fenn exploring the neighbourhood with his terrier.

Julia made off across the fields with the children, and the school in general spread themselves over the country-side, trespassing or not according to taste.

Nigel and Johnny went down the hill together, and through the village, their Sunday straws tilted over their noses. They overtook Kedge's underlings ambling down towards the great high road running through the valley to the West, where it was their Sabbath habit to sit in the ditch and spit and watch the cars go by.

Beyond the village burial ground Nigel turned off down a track to the marshes; and there among the reeds and dykes they steeped their trousers in mud.

Nigel spoke strongly about Sunday uniform. "The Proprietor," he said, speaking of the Headmaster, "must have an aspidistra outlook to go on making us wear shop-walkers' clothes on a country ramble."

And Johnny said that if he were a Headmaster he'd have a Continental Sunday with ordinary games, and revelry, and the O.T.C. band playing, and then there'd be no poaching around, and bursting through hedges and chivying sheep, and all the rest of the things that William said the farmers and keepers came to him about.

" But then we'd not get out of the asylum the

whole term through," said Nigel ; " as it is, once a week is precious little to get out of a community. I don't count trips down the village. William says there's only one thing better than going out by yourself, and that's staying at home alone in the house."

Johnny said he thought William should go away and live in a tub. " But we," he added, " should have a cache of filthy tweeds in a haystack, and just come and change on Sundays, and then we could cut ourselves sticks and loll in the ditches, or go into the woods and pretend we were keepers ; and send thousands of names in to the house-masters."

But Nigel said that Sunday was no day for deception. There were too many people about with their eyes open and nothing to do.

He broke into a trot, bounding away over a stretch of half-drained swamp with Johnny at his heels.

They came to a bridge over a dyke, with a gate in the middle, and beyond, a field with black and white cows lying down.

" It's going to rain," said Johnny.

But of this there was no sign. Rather, the morning's sullen lack of colour had gone, and there was a crescent glow in the air, and a warmth of approaching sunlight through the haze, that gave vividness to the faint grey-greens of the marsh lands, and behind a line of willows the village spire " dressed itself," as Frog would say, against the sky.

There came to them a sound of bells, a clanging murmur.

From the heart of the swamp birds called harshly and there was a warm smell of grasses and water weeds ; a rich place clamorous with marsh life ; muffled, coming to them out of the quiet and the haze ; thriving, unchanging and remote from mankind.

Nigel fanned himself with his hat, and Johnny said the colours of the place reminded him of home. For some time they sat on the gate talking, and Johnny took a stick to poke away the mud from underneath his heels.

They came back into the House as the bell was ringing for tea, and afterwards Gray called Johnny into his study.

Johnny, who had set aside the hour between tea and Chapel to write to Mark, followed Gray and festered with rage.

" See here, my good boy," said Gray, " I want you to do something for me every evening until I tell you to stop."

Johnny looked down sourly at his feet.

" I want you," continued Gray, " to rid my study of flies. I hate flies ; they nauseate me, especially in Autumn when they're slow and sticky, and I won't have them settling down here for the night, all over my ceiling. I'll show you how to deal with them. Mark me."

He went to a corner and fetched a strange contrivance. It was a bamboo pole, some four feet in length, to which was lashed the head and stem

of a wine glass. The base had been broken away.
Johnny grew interested. Gray then took a bottle
from his mantelpiece and filled the wine glass with
a mauve liquid.

" Now," he said, " you want to wait till after
sundown, when they're all parked for the night.
Then you lift this pole very stealthily on high, and
trap the foul and pestilent creatures against the
ceiling." So speaking he did this with infinite care,
imprisoning the flies one by one, and dazed by the
fumes of the methylated spirit, they fell down and
drowned in the wine glass.

Gray caught five flies and Johnny begged to be
allowed to try. He caught two and startled one
away. Then Gray finished for him. Their joint bag
was eleven flies and a daddy-long-legs. The corpses
with their legs wrapped about them in their death-
agonies looked like currants, swaying gently as Gray
lowered the pole.

He then undid the wine glass and taking a scrap
of muslin strained the methylated spirit through a
funnel, back into its bottle, and flicked the corpses
out of the window.

The fly-season lasted from May till November, he
reckoned, and he kept count of the number caught,
jotting it down upon a sheet of squared paper. On
Saturday nights he joined seven dots together with
red ink, and this graph hung upon his walls, and
thus did he waste his time.

He told Johnny that at the end of October he
would be sending the season's statistics up to the
Governors with a request that they should look to

the sanitation of the House. It was not William's
fault, it was the geographical position of his study
he said, giving as it did upon the courtyard. And
Johnny agreed that it was certainly the proximity
of William's kitchens that attracted the flies. He
thanked Gray for the demonstration, and with this
entrancing sport in view, went off to tell Mark all
about it in a hasty letter.

Evening Chapel was at half-past six, preceded by
House call-over. Johnny, with those of his size
from his own and other Houses, came into a building
empty save for the Housemasters' wives already
installed.

A prefect stood on the chancel steps ; at a great
distance he seemed, and beyond him was the
altar with candles shining steadily, a pale fair
light.

Johnny followed the boy in front right up the
nave and sat down beside him.

And up the nave the stream continued, and the
noise of feet upon stone. Bench after bench silted
up ; and still they came, unsmiling and unhurried,
growing larger and larger. Johnny, dazed, watched
them from the lowest bench.

It so happened that he missed the modest entry
of Gray and Nigel (who appeared amongst those
like themselves, who were House prefects
but not school prefects), on the heels of those
members of the Sixth Form who were not prefects
at all.

Now all the while the organ pealed ; Bach it was,
and high up in the organ loft there was light and a

music-master's cranium shone, and was reflected in a little mirror.

Then came the junior masters. One or two looked hot and prickly, Johnny thought, and gazed elaborately at the vaulting or elaborately down at their toes, neither of which directions seemed to afford them any comfort in their embarrassment. The man Fenn swept past his nose in a fine rabbit hood, but he looked indifferent and calm. These younger men were followed by other masters, and Johnny picked out that well-nourished Frog, who was a Protestant.

Then came the Housemasters, nine of them, and William in amongst them, who *would* hold his mortar-board by the tassel. Teacher stepped alongside of him.

The organ made an end and there was a pause, utterly silent. Then the ten school prefects entered, and with a mighty rumble the school stood. Lastly came the Headmaster and the Senior Prefect who shut him into his stall. The Headmaster was a man of height and breadth of shoulder; of an unhurried glance and deliberate gesture. He had a low voice with many tones in it and a rugged ugly face. This man had the affection of his staff without scavenging round for it; and although he used his prefects to their fullest, he never let them come between him and the masters.

Looking him over Johnny wondered, and in a dream he prayed and sat and sang and stood.

Half-way through the Magnificat he located Gray and his brother high up in the choir. Above their heads were names upon the wall, blurred in the distance ; Crimea names, Boer War names, and further along those of the Great War—panel after panel, already mellowing with the years.

The service progressed, and by and by they turned to the East and it was twilight.

The gathering darkness stole all colour from the window. The glass was pale as moths' wings, and the lead divisions, delicately traced, stood out as branches on a sunless sky.

By the time the Proprietor stood at the lectern for his first sermon of the year, the lights were lit, and the sky darkened to a burning blue, against which the lead divisions glistened as though a snail had passed. For just ten minutes the Headmaster spoke of self-discipline.

He spoke tersely and his words were memorable.

There was a silent attention.

But Johnny felt sick.

It came on suddenly, scattering his thoughts. He was hot and cold. " It isn't me. It isn't true. I don't feel sick. It's a nasty dream. I shall wake up out of it. I couldn't possibly be sick here, it would ruin my life."

Was there no help ? His cry went up, How long ? But the sermon continued.

No. He must fight this out privately. He shut his eyes. As he dare not go out of Chapel in the flesh, he would in spirit quit the building.

And so, breathing shakily, he did. Right down the nave and out of the west doors to lie in the grass and breathe and breathe out there in the darkness. . . .

Then he knew he was safe. He'd won.

It was all right. He wasn't going to be sick. He felt perfectly well, and the sermon ended at the same time.

He rose and stood triumphant as the Proprietor returned to his stall.

But perhaps it would be as well not to risk singing the hymn.

CHAPTER V

"The time for rat-catching arrived at last and the hunt began."—THOMAS HARDY.

BOTH William and Gray were pleased. For William had heard by the morning post that a relative had named him residuary legatee ; and so despite a cold in the head he was in fine fettle.

As for Gray, he was that morning after school elected Captain of the House XV. The Selection Committee met in William's study. It consisted of William, his prefects, three old colours, one or two of the younger masters ; and Benjamin Kettle, the school sergeant, a magnificent man of rolling muscle and a concave stomach.

In every other House the election took place at the end of the summer term ; but William liked to have this little flutter in September ; and to-day it had passed off without a hitch, William smiling and telling Gray in candid friendliness that it was against his better judgment. Gray smiled back and was still smiling when he dropped into Nigel's study sometime later.

But Nigel would have him know that his position was in no way due to any skill he had acquired at the game in recent years ; but rather to those gifts Nature had given him. " For," he said, " just as fish have fins, birds wings, and pigs snouts, so you have a low centre of gravity, great speed, cabriole legs and the reach of an ape."

And Gray did not dispute it. Smiling proudly he took a turn round the study, and then sat down in Nigel's arm-chair with his hands behind his head and his cabriole legs curving over the side.

" I'm not going to waste my time over you elderly muscle-bound boys," he said. " You must just go through with your usual rough, coarse, scalping game." And he spoke of new cloth and old garments ; of new wine and old bottles. " But," he concluded, " the colts shall be taught to play the game as it should be played. I shall take them once a week myself and Fenn shall do the rest. He was a Greyhound, I'm told. And I shall ask William if they need watch Second XV matches ; it's a shocking waste of time."

" William won't let them off unless other Houses do," Nigel pointed out.

" Oh, yes he will, out of pure perversity. I'll manage him. Besides, he's often said he hates an undergrowth of younger boys, frozen and sneezing on the touch-line."

" Well," said Nigel, " it's no good hurrying, with the grounds like concrete. I heard Kettle telling Fenn they shouldn't have played on Saturday. Other Houses had runs."

Gray said that Kettle had missed his vocation and should have been a male nurse.

He reached down Nigel's calendar and perused the match fixtures, glancing over lectures and recitals as well. Then he felt for a pencil and ticked off " Sermon by Headmaster," which came first on the list.

School calendars were of cardboard and shaped like the roof of a house, or the Bill of Fare at a restaurant, so they might stand on study mantel-pieces. The arrangements for the first half of the term were on one side, and those until Break-up on the other. Half-term was marked in red ink at the crease.

To the printed list Gray added his own and William's birthday. For they shared the 10th of October ; and William, discovering this, had given Gray half-a-crown for the first three years. Also Gray marked Guy Fawkes' Day, and then in-serted " Rat Day " between the Headmaster's first sermon and a lecture on " Colonisation." " Rat Day " was a function peculiar to William's House, and was to take place that very after-noon.

This annual fixture preceded " National Rat Week " by about a month, and the date was chosen by Simon Kedge, who had to make arrangements in the village and round about for his friends to bring their dogs and ferrets.

The ratting took place in the early afternoon down by the pigsties. Kedge had his friends and his underlings, and William's prefects invited those from other houses and certain of the younger masters, and no one else.

Any boy found near the pigsties was twice beaten—for being out of bounds in William's vegetable gardens, and for seeing prefects off their guard.

This afternoon, William, who usually went to the ratting, was unable to do so on account of his cold.

Julia forbade it. After lunch, or rather school dinner, she led him into his study, put him into his chair and lit a fire. Then she fetched his big warm overcoat, with its poacher pockets, and having put it about his shoulders, opened the windows.

" You must be careful, William, to keep warm and keep away from us all, and try not to give it to the children."

William was unable to answer ; he was trembling in a delicious agony on the brink of a sneeze. But he waved wildly at her as he hunted desperately through his pockets for a handkerchief. He found one just in time, and exploded violently into it.

And down by the pigsties they waited in the sun. The day was bright and cool and already the topmost twigs were bare. It was as yet early. A fringe of boys hung over the pigsties, passing remarks on William's porkers and gently scratching their backs for them.

The air was full of smells.

There was the rich smell of pigsty and the

bitter smell of chrysanthemums in pots, waiting in Kedge's wheelbarrow to be taken into the house.

And besides that a whiff of tar brought out by the sun, for the sties had been repainted for the winter.

Then, too, there were the fleeting smells of earth and of the leaves underfoot, besides the dustiness of cinders kicked aside, that caught in the throat ; and the heavy aromas of those rat-infested mounds ; half rubbish-heap, half marrow-beds behind the lilac bushes, which were to provide the day's sport. Down at the farther end of the cinder track the lime trees tossed in the wind ; but under the wall by the pigsties there was shelter and a steady warmth.

Ranged against the wall were old tennis posts and planks from a greenhouse that had been pulled down. They were cracked and the paint was flecking off them. Farther along were scout poles, roughened by the weather, and bundles of pea-sticks and raspberry-canes stacked in a corner, and great swathes of netting for the red currants, which week by week, as they caught his eye, prompted Kedge to remind himself to put them away under cover for the winter.

At length Nigel and Gray arrived with Penhurst and others. They came up whistling, their feet crunching upon the cinder path. They wore flannels pale with age and spotted. Their sweaters were dim.

Gray wore besides, a scrum-cap, and Nigel a

66

sun-bonnet of Lavender's, much faded, which had
been packed by mistake in his box.

Although they had never before assisted at a
Rat Day, they seemed at home.

Pushing their way into the crowd round the sty,
they caught hold of one Taunton, Captain of
Throssell's House, swung him up off his feet and
down amongst the pigs.   To save himself, Taunton
clutched hold of a hairy pink back below ; but it
fled, squealing, away.   Taunton cried aloud, and
red and gasping, was hauled back out of the mud
and stenches into safety.

When he turned round, the scrum-cap and sun-
bonnet were far away, larking with Kedge's wheelbarrow.   They tossed out the chrysanthemums and
gave each other rides.

They rumbled in and out of the crowd, and
then dashed away down the cinder path, scattering the main body of Kedge's companions, who
were even now arriving, spitting to right and
to left, their trousers caught up with string,
their   mongrels   yapping   under   their   feet ;
mongrels sniffing the cinders and stiff with
anticipation.

And there were ferrets in sacks, twitching ; and
the men's rough clothes seemed part of the landscape, seasoned and mellowed as the walls and
trunks of the trees.   They drew aside with Kedge,
who stood in the door of a potting-shed, hand on
hip, knee bent, his lanthorn face creased with the
worry of keeping an eye on all the young gentlemen at once.   By this time both Nigel and Gray

were in his wheelbarrow. (It was a deep wheelbarrow, with extra boards let into grooves on all four sides.) Trundled by their friends, they passed at speed through a grove of prefects, who lashed at them with scarves as they went by.

Imperturbable, they bowed first to one side and then to the other in a distinguished sort of way; and Nigel kept lifting his sun-bonnet. On the return journey they were tumbrilled aristocrats, their arms about each other, gazing with fortitude up into the clouds.

But opposite Kedge's dunghill, a superb midden built up against the wall, they were thrown out maliciously on to the cinders, and only just missed rolling up against the lower slopes of the manure heap.

This sobered them and they ceased their clowning. Recovering their breath, they felt they would like to have a look at Kedge's parrot.

This bird was commonly called " Polly Minor," as opposed to plain " Polly," who was Miss Greig; but Nigel always referred to it as " our foul-mouthed feathered friend." For all that, it was a pure bird and couldn't say a word. Kedge kept it by him for company during the day, and took it home to his cottage in the evening. Nigel and Gray peered at it through the window of the potting-shed.

In an earth-smelling twilight it swung, a dim green on its perch. And as they tapped the glass and squarked and chirruped at it, the poor bird rolled a silly eye in silence and flapped its faded wings in the gloom.

A few minutes later John Fenn came up, in the dirtiest flannels of all, with his terrier panting *ventre à terre* in a harness calculated to transfer all strain from neck to shoulders. Excited by the noise and crowd, this terrier sang and coughed, pawing the cinders.

Fenn had to pick him up. When he let him go, reaching the arena in front of the pigsties, Tim sped away and went lovingly for Gray's trousers.

With a cry, Gray leapt high in the air, and this pandemonium roused the worst passions of the other mongrels, who began to advance upon one another, quivering. Suddenly the spell was broken, and two trundle-tailed brutes, unspeakable and spotted, upped and leapt one upon the other with hideous noise, and fought inextricably with dovetailed jaws.

Others joined them.

Kedge's companions, who up till now had stood in a phlegmatic cluster, stumbled forward with oaths to sort their dogs.

Wading in, they pulled three unlovely quadrupeds apart. The disturbance was indescribable, and to top it all, Tim went and got his hind legs entangled in the netting by the wall, and set up his yelping anew. Nigel, sick with laughter and blinded by his sun-bonnet, lurched backward into one of Kedge's underlings, and the two of them, overbalancing, fell among the planks, dislodging a pile of seed-boxes.

The crowd surged about them and a ferret got loose.

Then there was a roar : the first rat appeared, a desperate shadow glancing along the wall. Never had there been such a Rat Day !

Nigel, who held views as to happiness being solely a matter of anticipation and memory, lived in the moment, bellowing in a fine perspiration, his sun-bonnet hanging down his back.

And during the wild hunt that followed he became convinced there was nothing in the world to touch ratting, unless it were that ragging in Form which had made his rosy past.

These sports run each other close.

About four o'clock the dogs were called off, the dead rats assembled and counted, and ferrets put away tenderly into their sacks.

Grimy and heated, the prefects returned to their Houses.

Kedge went off down the hill with his companions and their dogs. At his cottage he parted from them, hung the parrot's cage upon its hook, had a bit of tea with his wife, and later came out on to the road again and lit his pipe. There was a nip in the air. In the valley lights appeared, winking.

Simon started down the hill, turned up his collar and quickened his pace.

With every step he took he felt a bigger man. For although he might cut a poor figure in William's and Mrs. Turvey's eyes, he was very highly thought of down in the village, and at the ' King's Arms,' whither he was bound, and where he was known as

" Mr. Kedge wot works up at Dean's." And as he opened the Bar Parlour door the warmth and smoke and beery cosiness enfolded him; and outside the Bar Parlour curtains the sun went down, a red ball behind the trees.

CHAPTER VI

" Rational explanation is an intellectual luxury."
—LANFRANC'S OPINION.

WILLIAM was hard at work teaching elementary mathematics. He stood at the blackboard working out a simple equation, writing fast and boldly.

He was not using his own brain. That would have been a simple matter; as easy as winking or falling off a log, or any other of these superlatively facile things. Instead, he drew on the intelligence of his pupils; so scanty; pouncing with apparent indiscrimination amongst them, and panting at the strain and labour of extracting whatever meagre information they had to give.

The boys leapt up when questioned, and quickened by fear and William's electric personality, gave answers they felt to be inspired; and sat down sweating.

All except Johnny. He sat cold and his brain was numb. He was by now past caring what happened on the blackboard. His throat ached and his eyes felt hot in their sockets. He kept them fixed on William's head, which, shining in the sun, looked neither fair nor faded, but just bright.

Johnny heard nothing. He understood nothing, having for some time lost all track of William's reasonings; and he felt that should William's diabolical finger point at *him*, he should just curl up and die. Figures were indeed the invention of the devil. And on the blackboard William's equation was coming out. In Johnny's eyes its blurred and dizzy shape was fast tapering to a point; and finally William wrote: $x = \dfrac{4 \cdot 2}{5}$ and worked it to three sig. figs.

"There you are," he said triumphantly, and flapped a yellow duster, and the chalk dust danced in the sun. "And now," he said, glancing at the clock, "you've just time to do one for yourselves. Turn to page 50, No. 47b."

A faint, unhappy sigh passed through the room, and there was a fluttering of leaves.

William spoke again: "First," he said, "let me warn you of one thing. In the old days when I was young and did mathematical examples, it was an understood thing between the author of the sum, myself, and the man who set it, that it should work out to a decent round Christian number. But now the modern fashion is all for giving you faith in your method; and modern answers are frequently some fraction so cumbrous and strange as to arouse suspicion. But, as I say, with a clear conscience and faith in your method, nothing need alarm you.

"Now, judging from my result on the board, this Mr. What-Ever-He-Calls-Himself " (and William

perused the back of his textbook) " is probably
up to these tricks ; but of course," and here he
dropped his voice with some solemnity, " he may
be such a subtle fellow that he goes one better
and springs a whole number on you in double bluff !
So be careful, and don't let me find any boy copying
it down wrong to start with.

" Now get on with it." And he sat down at his
desk.

Slowly Johnny copied the thing down in misery,
and began to broach it.

After a little while he realised in a weary despair
that the accursed thing was expanding, instead of
contracting. Each line he wrote was longer and
more intricate than the last, a labyrinth of x's
and y's.

He went back and searched for faults. His
reasoning seemed to him quite flawless. So he sat
with blind eyes fixed on his paper, and his gorge
rose at the thought of the evening's preparation.
In doing work for William he gleaned information
from any source he could. He cared not a fig for
marks, honourable or illicit ; but yearned to finish
and get the stuff off his mind. He suffered torture
in William's lessons. They were four times a week,
and it wasn't even the end of October.

His worst moments came when, after an explanation, William would look round and say : " Now
is there any boy who has not understood ? I will
go no further unless every boy is clear. Is every
boy clear ? "

And then would come a conventional pause, a

brief silence, resembling that which follows the
giving out of marriage banns ; and as rarely
broken ; whilst every boy looked round upon every
other boy superciliously, to see if there was amongst
them any boy fool enough not to have understood.
On these occasions Johnny drew himself up and
gave glance for glance, bringing " that willing
suspension of disbelief " to bear on the matter in
hand. And now, praying the bell would release
him, he sat on, very stiff and sorrowful, with his
pen poised over the paper as if, with every confidence in his method, he was just about to write
something down.

Then William's voice cut across the heavy-
breathing silence :

" Bentley, bring your work and come up
here."

Johnny, feeling sick, came up to the daïs, and
William went through the expanding tangle. Quite
soon his finger came to rest. He looked up
accusingly at Johnny beside him.

" And look what you've done," he said in tones
of horror.

Johnny glanced down with distaste at his handi-
work. Yes, there was certainly a blemish, some
little matter of a minus and the removal of a bracket ;
and William said curtly, tapping the page :

" Surely you know enough to change these signs
in here ? "

Johnny clenched his hands. He was in torment.
And William, perceiving his face, dropped his
voice.

75

" See here," he said confidentially, " you'll understand all this in time ; but for the present you just take it from me that it's most unheard-of not to change these signs. It simply isn't done." And he added with a twinkle that it was as bad as brown boots with a bowler.

" And then," as Johnny told Nigel afterwards with his favourite simile, " me spirits rose sudden like boiling milk, and as I went back to me seat that bloody bell rang, and about time, too."

That afternoon Nigel went to tea with William. He came in late. The long oval table was surrounded, and there appeared to be no vacant seat for him. He stood looking about, feeling like the odd man at musical chairs ; and William said :

" Come along, you can squeeze in beside me. There's a chair by the wall," and he jerked an outcurving thumb towards covered dishes on the hearth.

Nigel took a plate and a knife from the sideboard, and inserted himself between William and Penhurst, sitting with elbows drawn into his ribs. On the other side of William was Taunton, whom they had tossed three weeks ago into the pigsty. Beyond him Fenn and then Gray, with his face in his teacup, which he tilted to get at the sugar.

On Gray's left sat Polly, brisk in bottle-green, and Mrs. Dean at the head of the table, who was pouring out his tea. With the milk-jug in her hand she looked down the table and raised her eyebrows. Nigel nodded. Then pointing at the sugar, she lifted a finger. Nigel, smiling politely, put up two. Like Gray, he was fond of sugar. Down came his cup from hand to hand, unsteadily, past one of Throssell's prefects and one of Warner's and one from the School House, a grim creature, captain of Runs, to Penhurst, who put it down in front of Nigel's plate.

The room was lit by candles on the table and the unwavering glow from the fire.

Above the fire-place there hung a little Flemish Madonna, with pale-red hair and high forehead. And at her feet in miniature, the patroness of the picture, kneeling amongst prim flowers. The table was stacked with food of Mrs. Turvey's making, for Polly and Julia agreed that if boys were asked to tea they must be filled as full as they would fill themselves in studies or in the dining hall.

From time to time the master of the House made gestures towards this or that cake, without restraining his flow of talk. When Nigel came in William was about half-way through a rhetorical tirade against what he was pleased to call 'the Ruination of Associations.' It was some casual mention of Twickenham that set him off.

"Twickenham!" he growled, and there was in his face that uncertainty between gloom and hilarity that made it inadvisable to smile. "Twickenham! That arena of the Muddied Oaf. And to think that Pope once lived and wrote there. And Stoke Poges, where Gray wrote the 'Elegy,' overrun with golfers. Athletics spreading over holy names. Look at the Achilles and the Corinthians ! " And that, he would have them note, was as nothing compared with what had been done in trade.

" Why ! " he cried in rising indignation, " I get up in the morning to find the sacred name of Erasmus twisted round my shaving soap in adjectival form ; and the next thing that catches my eye is a bottle of hygienic fluid called after the author of ' Paradise Lost ' ; and then when I turn away flinching, it is to climb into my winter under-wear stamped with the disgusted face of Cardinal Wolsey ! "

He lowered his head into his hands.

This glimpse of William dressing upset Nigel. He caught Gray's eye, saw the faces of others twitching, bright and carefully restrained ; and Polly's purple visage ; and he began to shake. Penhurst kicked him hard, but he was too far gone, and seizing his teacup drank, and drinking choked, and choking drowned all conversation.

When he recovered they were talking about the construction of novels and character-drawing. Fenn said it would be hard enough to make characters live, but to make them die convincingly was next door to an impossibility, he thought. And Polly said that that was just what she was going to say.

Gray asked her if she had noticed a tendency to remove them with cancer. It seemed to have replaced the Victorian decline. Polly stiffened.

" Once," said William, coming out of a dream,

" I wrote a book.   But the hero was so intellectual that I couldn't arrange for him to open his mouth. And there it ended."

He gave a great sigh and rose from the table.

Later he retained Nigel in his study.

" I've been talking to Mr. Throssell about you and your Oxford plans," he said.   " From him I gather that your final choice is now narrowed down to Greats, History, Forestry, Agriculture or Law. Mr. Throssell and I were wondering what exactly you are thinking of taking when you go up for a scholarship in March.   Also there seems to be some mystery as to what work you are doing at the moment.   Mr. Throssell said, moreover, that he'd heard you were taking Responsions in December. It is to be hoped you get through the whole at once, and don't take it portion by portion.   I suppose it was an oversight that you didn't take it last year.   Mark you, this is only idle curiosity. I've not yet seen Mr. Cardington.   I expect to him and you these things are clear."   Cardington was Sixth Form master.

Under these sarcasms Nigel tried to clear his head, saying with truth that there was nothing he had not considered.   Yes, he was taking Responsions in December, and hoped to be let in on his Classical scholarship papers in March, or was it April ?

After that he had thought of doing English Literature, only Mr. Cardington said it was a narrow school, and his father wanted him to read Greats.   History had been in the air, with a view to research afterwards, and a travelling grant in a foreign land. But he wasn't good enough. Law he had heard was sound in case of business, and he had once mentioned Agriculture to Mr. Throssell, years ago, because he fancied the open air and time to read as well.

" You wouldn't have time to read if you made it pay," said William, and told of a family who kept a poultry farm at a slight loss, and were out from cockcrow till dusk, when they came in to wash eggs, until, blind with fatigue, they stumbled off to bed to snatch a few hours' sleep before getting up to sit beside their incubators.

And he was just going on with another anecdote about a man who went in for forestry and, sitting on a bough, sawed it off between himself and the tree-trunk, when Nigel said :

" How about Modern Greats, sir ? "

William, showing no surprise at yet another proposition, said : " You must decide for yourself, otherwise you'll have a grievance against me. Now I think we've mentioned everything bar Economics and Modern Languages. If you think of anything else come and tell me." He smiled and said he would see Mr. Cardington. Then suddenly he dropped this banter. " You don't read enough," he said, and looked at Nigel with distance and speculation in his eyes. " If you've done with that biography I should like it for Penhurst, and you can choose something else." For a stream of new books passed constantly through William's house— biographies, memoirs, modern poetry, books of

travel, essays and certain novels ; and these he lent
to the Sixth and Fifth Forms in his House ; insti-
tuting a lending library, quite apart from the
House library used by junior boys. And he kept
himself informed as to who were reading what ;
taking particular pains with those boys on the
modern side. But Nigel passed by the pile of
recently published books, and, his eyes moving up
and down upon the shelves, he arrived in a corner
by the piano and singled out one of William's
prizes—certain of Hazlitt's Essays, bound up in
calf, with a golden crest. William approved his
choice. A good man, Hazlitt, he said, and aware
of his limitations. And he wrote with zest.
William, moreover, liked his painter's eye ; so
vivid. An unsuccessful painter, of course, but a
shrewd and plucky man, and a brisk quarreller.

If writers hadn't got a trade, said William, they
should at least have a working knowledge of another
art, to enlarge their horizon and reduce their self-
esteem.

" You read that bit about the Indian jugglers,"
he counselled ; " there's a description of a man
playing fives ; and remarks on fives in general.
Very tasty."

Nigel went off with Hazlitt under his arm, and
dropped in on Gray to chat about careers.

Gray was not helpful. Like all his male for-
bears, he was going into the army, and understood
nothing of choice or indecision.

And in his study William sat down to slash at
exercises.

A maid came in to draw the curtains, and after her the children, to say good night.

Then he was left alone.

A log hissed. The firelight gleamed on the parquet. Outside was a rumble of wheels on the hill.

CHAPTER VII

> " . . . O thou
> Who chariotest to their dark wintry bed
> The wingéd seeds, where they lie cold and low,
> Each like a corpse within its grave, until
> Thine azure sister of the Spring shall blow
> Her clarion o'er the dreaming earth, and fill
> With living hues and odours plain and hill."
> —Shelley.

THE wind was high and blowing strongly from the West—Shelley's wind, deep and reverberating.

It was one of those wild, shining, untidy days, when the very air seems polished ; a day of fast-moving skies, and the high clouds blazing ; a day of leaning spires. Along the roads, wind-dried, the leaves were driven, crisp and with a hasty whisper ; and the birds, poor fowls, were shouting as though it were Spring. And they were not deluded, for there was an urge and a pulse in this wind, foretelling Spring.

Yet it was Autumn, for the soughing trees were stripped. The two were as one, for the year's re-birth now happened in its death ; and happened in this wind. So there was life and wheeling change ; and life was vivid and tempestuous.

83

More especially was it tempestuous in William's kitchen, for Mrs. Turvey, that sub-normal soul, puzzled by the noise and booming, stepped into the courtyard to see what it was all about.

The mad wind caught her Isabella-coloured cap, and she fled away indoors, crying out that she didn't know what things were coming to, with a tempest fit to blow the features off your face. Like the end of the world it was, she said, and Doomsday, a constant thought, took possession of her. Like Peter Damiani, she could not withdraw the eyes of her mind from her tomb.

But to-day she cheered up a little, and smacked her lips over the " many mansions."

And, moreover, there were other consolations. To the servants assembled to eat their heads off at eleven o'clock, she said with a blazing circular glance :

" Yes. Threescore years and ten, and then away we all go to nice consecrated ground—all except chapel folk and—murderers ! "

And she took a great breath, wiping her hands sanctimoniously upon an apron the colour of sheep in Hyde Park ; and stood serene in an atmosphere of ruffled Primitive Methodism. For she was C. of E.

A good many of these chapel folk, outraged, rushed from the kitchen in a body to give notice to anyone in authority they should meet.

The kitchen door swung loose upon its hinges, and a smell of artichokes escaped into the passage. The kitchen door hung loose owing to that cracking of crab's claws in the hinges, so hard to put a stop to. And the aperture was growing. Soon it would be wide enough for walnuts.

That afternoon Gray went out to coach his colts. For one reason or another he had been prevented from so doing until now. There was need for haste, for the first round of the junior House matches was due in ten days' time, and Fenn, who had drawn up a probable XV for Gray's inspection, was by no means satisfied. They were a sticky lot, he said, and went off for a walk with Clovis-Abel de Mesière. They could not play golf on account of the wind.

Gray had arranged with a scratch XV to come down from Warner's House to oppose his colts, and he walked across the Duds' Pitch towards the assembled players, in fine feather, elated by the weather and his official position.

Nigel, Penhurst and one or two more came with him just to have a look.

Gray started off in a burst of facetiousness, telling a small boy to shut the gate into the field on account of the draught. Then he went to the centre of the field, and bending down upon one knee crisply blew his whistle, and then blew it again savagely and went for a boy for being off-side.

They were a stagnant, flaccid lot of little boys, content with indifferent footwork and messy passes. So far Fenn had been unable to move them to greater things.

But Gray set about them from the first minute, and running fiercely amongst them, cried aloud most passionately, and told them what he thought

of them. And his remarks, now faint, now clear, were
borne on the wind to the watchers on the touch-line.

Bawling, he deplored the three-quarters' octo-
genarian shamblings. And he spoke a little to the
back about his dithering. The folk-dancing bon-
homie of the " line-outs " incensed him. The scrum
also gave him trouble. It meant so well and pressed
so low that it invariably collapsed in moribund
fashion, and Gray, not waiting for a general dis-
entanglement, picked one small boy off another
and shook it, for ever talking ; so that Nigel and
company were put in mind of the dog-fight on
Rat Day.

It was about this time that William, attracted
afar off by the noise and mirth of the spectators,
came up to windward, and with him a parent he was
showing round. It was unfortunate that he should
arrive in time to hear Gray's remarks ; and that
the parent, instead of listening to William's earnest
protestations as to the wind being cold and the tea
ready (which was improbable, as it was not yet
3.30), should have lingered in a startled fascination,
murmuring : " A very unorthodox coach ! "

And then Tim appeared in view, bearing up against
the West wind, which had blown his ears inside out.
Having lost Clovis-Abel and his master, he had
made his way home across the fields, and now
ran about yelping, until Nigel caught him up and
buttoned him inside his coat, whence he looked out
upon the game, panting and a-tremble. Then
Nigel and Penhurst took him away with them back
to the house.

The game continued, and towards the end the standard of play had improved beyond belief, and Gray's remarks became rather more instructional and less abusive. At the end he told them they were shaping well, but that they had a long way to go before the House-matches.

As it was, when the time came they reached the final, and but for a couple of knees with water on them and a mild case of ringworm, would have carried off the Colts' Silver Tankard; and Gray was well content.

And now he turned away and put on his coat. He walked back across the cricket field, silent at last; and the House stood out darkly against a flaming sky.

The Colts straggled behind with the wind booming in their ears, and in the Changing-room they discussed Gray and his ways.

Gray himself went to his study, made up the fire, and then stepped along to the dining hall. There was nothing for him in the letter-rack, and as he turned away he found the manservant at his elbow, who said that Mr. Dean would like to see him at once.

He went in to William glowing, and came out seething ten minutes later. He burst into Nigel's study, to find him with Penhurst, reading before a leaping fire. His wrath and agitation did not surprise them.

Penhurst said: " We were expecting you."

Nigel crooned: " And what has William been saying to my sweet to vex him so? You

naughty little unorthodox coach," and prodded
his diaphragm.

"Saying to me!" Gray muttered, and then
pulled himself together and told them *oratio recta*
and with gesture what exactly William had said.

At the close Penhurst told him he deserved it,
every word. "You shouldn't be so—er—volatile,"
he said in his deep voice.

(One could foresee Penhurst sitting in his Hall
surrounded by his dogs and grandchildren.) "It
was an unrestrained exhibition. We would have
said a word only we couldn't get at you. You never
looked at us, you kept running about and howling."

"Well, what would you have done with a lot of
little unspeakables whose passes went no faster
than an offertory-bag?" Gray scratched his ear
in a rising temper.

Nigel got up and pushed Gray into his chair.
Standing before the fire he toasted his trousers

"There's no need to make such a song and dance
of the affair," he said. "You should have told
William quietly that these passionate methods are
the natural outcome of living under his roof; and
that unconsciously you have moulded yourself on
him."

And as Gray's face began to brighten Nigel added :
"But it all goes to show that enthusiasm is a very
vulgar thing. And now will you both leave me?
I'm working till tea-time. William says I don't
work enough, and that I eat too much." So saying
he stretched, and his hands almost touched the
ceiling.

Then he opened the door for Gray and Penhurst ; shut it uncomfortably on their heels ; drew his curtains ; loosened his collar, and began hunting about in his bookshelves. All this foretold, maybe, great cerebral activity to come.

Johnny and a party of friends having changed after the game, collected their books for a period of history with Warner.

They went away up the road together towards the main school buildings ; walked, talked and jostled one another in the dusk, spry again after their shower baths. On arrival they sat down in their desks and stretched in delicious stiffness. Their faces burned, scorched by the wind.

When Warner, confound him, came in on the stroke of the hour, they got up and sat down again with grim faces. There was heavy work before them.

For Warner was one of those men who must at all costs be ' side-tracked.' He was most intolerably dull, with an iron discipline to boot ; and that enforced attention which he mistook for interest elated him ; inspiring further flights of boredom, enriched with many a cultured pleasantry.

Moreover he had that altogether criminal practice of setting too much preparation, and it was against this that his classes sought to guard themselves. For the amount of work set depended on the distance covered during the lesson. And the longer the man could be kept clearing up those little points that had arisen from last time's preparation, the less time he would have to cover new ground. For he set the preparation not from where he began, but from where he ended the lesson ; and expected a thorough knowledge of what he had dealt with during the hour itself.

And then he would settle on one boy and probe his ignorance with cruelty and pestering annoyance ; he had a way of saying : " And if not, why not ? " which was paralysing. When this happened a friend of the sufferer would suddenly appear to be bursting with information, and when asked to speak would give so soft an answer that Warner's wrath was turned away from his first victim, and by this counter-irritation they eased the pains of education.

Warner was moreover a brute of a man who asked written questions without regularity or warning ; indeed there was no peace of mind for anyone. So in face of a common enemy they were drawn together in a close fraternity to ' side-track ' him. O the art of ' side-tracking ' ! A subtle, ancient and necessary art.

And Warner, like many another, was never aware that it was being practised on *him*. He discerned nothing in the leading question, the eager glance and all that sawing the air with the hand.

Nor were his suspicions aroused by boys who, in their willingness to learn, and in their stupidity, begged him to go over that bit again ; nor by others who advanced alternative theories opening with : " I once read somewhere, Sir . . ." or : " I was always told as a child . . ." ; or the final gambit of : " What do you yourself think, Sir ? " which paved the way for what Warner had once thought—now maintained—and was prepared to believe.

Then there were those who, though just as keen to foster the lesson's procrastination, felt themselves unfitted to launch an argument. They usually rose up to say that they couldn't quite read what he'd written in the margin of their essays. Lastly there was a devoted remnant who could not trust themselves to speak at all ; but they were seized with nausea from time to time, and toothache ; and their noses bled opportunely ; and if, as on the present occasion, games were safely over, they even went so far as to feign a cricked neck and so create another glorious delay.

But this 'side-tracking' art was not to be mastered all in an instant. It was a craft requiring apprenticeship and patience, subtlety and confidence.

Very little was required of new boys beyond an occasional breakdown and a refusal to be comforted.

And to-night they sat row upon row, defending their interests, decoying the man Warner, and yearning for their tea.

The lights hanging low cast great cones of brightness, and above them the ceiling was dim. Through the uncurtained windows the sky showed purple and there was a sound of tossing trees. At that time they were immeshed in the French Revolution ; and at length they came to Marat in his bath.

And Johnny, who had a *flair* for ' side-tracking,' was just about to question the probability of a man like Marat having a bath, when he saw that the clock lacked but three minutes to the hour, and decided to save this ablutional theme for Warner's next lesson.

He loved ' side-tracking,' did Johnny, having heard speak of it at home, when Gray had come to stay. Gray had gone into the matter thoroughly for years, and never tired of recounting the incident of how Teacher, leading off a lesson with Lamb had, when the bell rang, arrived at the discussion as to whether or no tears were an asset to a married woman.

CHAPTER VIII

"Il faut avec rigueur ranger les jeunes gens."
—MOLIÈRE.

IT was November, and in Common Room Clovis-Abel stood limply waiting for the bell to ring.

His arms were full of grammars and vocabularies, which he held dolefully, as though they had been an ailing child, and he its mother, begging on some cold kerb.

So low was he that morning that he began to count his blessings. He was forty-three, had the air of less, and had diminished his weight by a kilo since the beginning of term.

But what was forty-three but another of those bleak milestones between the tingle of youth and the peace of old age? And of what account was this weight reduction, when it produced in him the hunger of a wolf, even for the unpalatable English food?

He sighed and passed on to other blessings.

The fact of his obtaining and keeping this post was in itself, he reflected, a matter for felicitation.

His compatriots, it would seem, did not flourish in these English schools. Always that question of discipline. But then the English discipline was so strange a thing, elusive and transcendent, independent of pomp and circumstance.

Once during his own school days he remembered that upon ink having been poured into the professor's hat, one had summoned the police.

But here it was not what one did, but what one was, that counted with these classes, who through one's actions discerned the panic through the bluff ; howsoever one might try to conceal it behind the loud voice and the lavish bestowal of punishment.

A little might be hid from one boy, but many boys together saw everything.

Now Clovis-Abel was not a vain man, and viewing his own lack of discipline with detachment, wondered why he was so little tormented in comparison with his poor friend Throssell for example.

But then his poor friend Throssell did not seem to care. He could forget, he could, and think of other things.

The real explanation lay in the fact that Teacher was ragged *actively* in his lessons. They set about him with hilarious disrespect and vain giggling ; it was a whole time job, and Teacher the focus of their activities. Whereas there was nothing in Clovis-Abel's personality to excite this. The Frog was ragged passively. They did exactly as they felt inclined, speaking when and to whom they chose, and there was no stint of laughter, for the sound of his maternal tongue ever struck comic to the ear ; but there was no community-aggravation of the man, so to speak. And in his lessons quite a lot of work was done ; not his work, it must be stated ; but at all events with him general education was not at so complete a standstill as it was with Throssell.

And Clovis-Abel thought about his friends, and a warmth stole into his heart.

This Throssell, who walked with him in France and turned a mediæval eye on the landscape ; who spoke poetry at him and nursed his English accent. And Warner, who took him out to hunt for flint arrowheads and gave him to understand the rudiments of heraldry, and showed him all his seals and documents.

And then there was this William, who lent him books, and talked and talked and talked and had him in to dinner, where the cooking was good ; and there was Mrs. Dean, who spoke French with such a charm, and played Chopin for him ; and Fenn as well, who knew Paris as the palm of his hand ; and the little dog who played with William's children, and sometimes had a bath and went into curl, so fluffy ! Ah ! he was beautiful, that little dog, with pretty ways, and yet he had no race, no race at all.

The only member of William's household who did not come in for his praise was Mary Greig ; but it was her own fault because she would cross-question him about the French Ministry and talked of Russian plays and the Stock Exchange, and sometimes philosophy. " Et que le ciel me défend," said Clovis-Abel, " d'une femme qui parle de la métaphysique ! "

The bell rang, cutting short these ponderings, and he went into school.

He found the young boys in their usual state, preoccupied and unprepared for him. There was an excitement in the air, for there was a match that afternoon.

The younger Bentley stood upon his desk waving a paper. For Johnny had been very much annoyed by the Frog's corrections of his 'unseen.' It had returned to him positively bleeding with red ink ; with a lot of bright red insults down at the bottom ; and Johnny climbed up before the Form to show what had been done ; as might a Roman general reveal his war-wounds to the multitude.

Seeing the Frog arrive, Johnny slipped down into his seat without embarrassment. And during the lesson he kept his eyes upon the man in a strange, bright stare ; and there was in his glance a devilry that unnerved Clovis-Abel.

The young boy appeared to listen, but was that probable ? And yet other masters too had noticed this attention. But not William. He said he found him in a quagmire of doubt and ignorance, both deaf and blind to all instruction. But in whatever Frog said he seemed absorbed. Not in the matter itself, Clovis-Abel was certain ; but rather for what it contributed to his thoughts. And now and then and suddenly he would drop his head and write a little, pressing eagerly with the pencil ; and then look up again with distant eyes in an alert dream, like a dog who sees movement away across a field and halts with an uplifted paw.

Then he would relax, as if returned from a long,
swift journey, and look freshly about the room ;
and start giving a lot of quiet trouble in his own
way.

For he would bank himself in with books upon
his desk, and jest with friends and neighbours ;
appearing to think that because the daïs was hidden
from him, that he was hidden from the master.
Like an ostrich he was, with its head in the sand.
Sometimes he would emerge to ask queer but
pertinent questions ; and Frog knew not what to
make of him.

But then he knew not what to make of any of
them.   And they in their turn did not try to make
anything of him.   He had been at this school a
year and a half ; and in that time he had, with his
pupils, worked up a fine atmosphere of reciprocal
distrust ; for in Clovis-Abel's classes, as in the
criminal courts of his dear country, one was guilty
until proved innocent.

With Throssell, William, Julia and Fenn, he felt
the glow of an international friendship based upon
common tastes ; but in Form he was a stranger
in a very strange land.   Sadly he went on with
his lesson.   Now it was expected that he should
teach certain things called Phonétiques ;   orally,
moreover ; and these, as far as he could see, were
nothing but a legitimate excuse for profuse and
unseemly noise.   He felt bitterly towards them,
undermining his discipline at the outset, as they did.

But those other members of the staff who taught
French swore by them, and he was overruled.

These others, Stratford-atte-Bowes all, were men of force and energy ; strong on paper ; with great chins, relentless mouths, and an incredible faculty for driving boys through their examinations.

One of them was a Rugger Blue, and he in speaking bruised the delicacies of the French language, as one might with clumsy fingers the bloom upon a plum.

And Clovis-Abel continued to write strange signs upon the blackboard ; and when he made a subtile nasal sound, and signed for the Form to do likewise, it was taken up mockingly, and turned into a monstrous bray !

The same day Nigel answered a letter from his father. He sat in his study with his feet on the mantelpiece. It was half-past twelve, and people returning to the House for dinner went by the window ; their voices grew and died away as did the sound of their footsteps.

Nigel wrote on steadily to counteract the feelings of his inside, for he was playing wing three-quarter for the School that afternoon.

He described his state to his father, whom he knew better on paper than in the flesh.

" My heart," he wrote, " seems to have sunk into my stomach and is beating heavily there. You know they put me into the XV early this term, and then tossed me out again for too much punting ahead. That was very painful. But now they're trying me this afternoon. Did you see what *The Times* said about our Three-quarters ? And do you realise that for this afternoon I am to be one of those superb creatures? If you knew how I felt, you'd put up a prayer for me. It's a perfect day; no wind and a neat grey sky. It's so still after these winds we've been having, and I feel incredibly brisk. There's still lunch to eat and an hour to wait, and then we'll get going."

He went on:

" Your younger son is, I think, perfectly happy, barring some discomfort over his maths. He played quite satisfactorily in a Colts' match yesterday. They led the School-house people a pretty dance, and William was as pleased as his nature would allow. Gray has been coaching them in his own queer way to some purpose. I went to tea with William about ten days ago. He told us exactly how he got up in the morning, and shocked poor Polly to the core. I choked. I did eat a lot. I like William's dining-room. Candles on the table and huge sad cakes, and the fire banked up red and quiet for toast.

" He has been at me again about my career, that man. Really, you know, I think I shall scribble down all the trades I can think of, and put them in a hat, and draw, and stick to whatever it turns out. So if you hear from William that I have at last decided to become a wart-charmer, you'll know how it came about.

" It's bad luck on you that there's no question of my being a doctor. You'll need someone to help you. Well, anyhow Johnny says he will be, at least for some years. I like people who know what they're going to do, like Gray. He's been going into the Army since before he was born. He has a military handbook which he knows by heart, and he quotes martial bye-laws, and keeps his hair cut in a short and soldierly fashion already. I tell him he shouldn't. But he and William's nasty little boy Andrew look like Institution brats. Now about that man Fenn. Are we really to have him for Christmas ? Has he no relations ? I don't think his mother should fling him into the bosom of our family. And why, when we live amongst them here, should we be cluttered up with ushers in the holidays ?

" But he's a nice man, new this term, straight from the 'Varsity. I forget his college. He's William's under-Housemaster. He's on the modern side. Chemistry, I think. But this is enough. The poor fellow won't have anything left to tell you himself. Personally I'd feel a fool to look so typically the Englishman as he does ; yellow hair and flax-blue eyes. But he has a cosmopolitan out-look, and goes about with our Frog.

" Did I tell you that he's got a dog. High and uncer-tain on its legs, with russet curls. It made a great disturb-ance on ' Rat-day.' He'll bring it with him. It's always with him. He practically takes it into Form with him. Johnny would be very pleased for the dog to come at Christmas. He's fond of it. It has a certain swerve when it runs which J. has copied, and swears that this is what got him into the Colts' XV !

" Now you ask about that Compton-Mallet youth. Where did Lavender meet him ? He left last year. He's just gone up to Oxford. Yes. We knew him very well. He was in this House, and gave William a lot of tepid trouble. Like me he could not decide what to do or be. So his papa took him up to London, they say, and had him psycho-analysed. You know, one of those places where they tap your scalp and tell your vocation. Well, they scratched his for him for three guineas, and then said he might be fit for clerical work ! Now don't you think we might do that these holidays ? Just you and I,

to set my mind at rest. We could go up and combine
the interview with a side-splitting pantomime. But they
aren't side-splitting any longer, are they? William says:
' All their rich vulgarity has passed away in favour of
dazzle and prettiness.' In any case I think I'd choose
something else. I think I'd rather go and have some
costly tragedy instead. Something on a large scale, I
think. A compound, say, of ' Hamlet,' ' Lear,' 'Othello,'
' The Meistersingers,' ' Phèdre ' and ' Dauber ' and ' The
Dynasts.' How about that? We must keep an eye
open.

"Oh, do find me a trade. I always feel ambitious in
the Autumn. Autumn's my own private Spring. Now
you mustn't think I'm boiling up to be a poet.

" I'm not like you and William, wailing amongst the
falling leaves. I always enjoy the way you bemoan the
' passing of summer,' my good man. Scowling at the mists
on the river. And then you go about with an air of sinister
cheerfulness, anticipating the autumnal disorders of your
patients, brought on by decaying vegetation as they think;
and you support their views and quote Theocritus, which
soothes and flatters them.

" I am now going to feed. Of *course* I'm short of money.
And when I tell you that Chapel collections grow heavier
each term, and that we're taxed out of existence, you'll
believe me.

" My love to Lavender and you."

Nigel sealed the letter without reading it, and
tore down the corridor with a flat indoor wind in
his face, and pulling up dead at the door of the
dining hall, passed up to the High Table in a stately
walk.

. . . (Next day Mark read his son's letter. Was it ten or twelve pages? And what chance was there for Nigel to settle down to the choice of a career with all this chitter-chatter in his head? Moreover—and he was sorry to say so—that letter was written with an eye on his biographer. Mark was not pleased.)

The Frog was famished, "décidément il se sentait un rude creux dans l'estomac," but he controlled himself and ate with elegance, making conversation with those boys on either side of him.

He sat at the head of one of the junior tables, and to his grief this accursed seat had been allotted to him twice a week throughout the term, for he was attached to William's House for dinner.

And there he sat, ill at ease, and appalled not so much by the ignorance of the talk around him, as by its flippancy.

And yet it was ignorant too, and grossly so. Until coming to this place he had always thought of ignorance as a simple negative thing; but now he saw it in its wantonness; positive and mischievous. Farther down the table sat Johnny; his eyes on the tablecloth behind his tumbler, magnified and coarsened by the water in the glass.

Cheerful noise went on about him. A hum of talk, the scrape of knife and fork, the piling of plates and the quick footsteps of servants between the tables.

Someone reaching for the salt jogged his arm. He sat up and looked about him, waiting for his food. In the hall, hung at suitable intervals upon William's red walls, were pictures, large and set in black oak frames; depicting such battles as Hastings, Bannockburn, Agincourt and the like; and Richard outside the walls of Chaluz; all very similar and colourful. The usual mediæval brawl, warriors cheek by jowl amongst the lances; very crude, thought Johnny.

William was indeed ashamed of them, and swore that directly he could afford to replace them they should go to adorn the walls of the Sick-house, and startle the malingerers there. But it was an awkward situation, for nothing smaller than a set of railway posters would cover the unfaded patches upon the walls.

However these battle-scenes gave a homely, almost nursery atmosphere to the dining hall, not to be despised.

Below the pictures there was panelling, and the fire-places were enclosed in circular guards, upon which junior boys sat, singeing their clothes, and the bars were bent and perpetually bright.

Afar off at the High Table upon a platform, William sat, flanked about by his House-prefects.

It was not known of what they talked, but now and then they laughed decorously together, and Johnny gazing, supposed them to be sucking humour from Higher Mathematics, and smiled bitterly.

And at that moment his food arrived.

He too, like Clovis-Abel, was hungry, but he put off eating in order to play the clown.

At once he said : " What have we here ? " and looked intently down into his plate, and lowered his nose into it.

He then began to recognise food that he had rejected yesterday ; morsels thrust aside last week and the week before, pointing them out to his friends with his fork.

And they leant over his plate and over their own, pointing too and exclaiming.

Johnny chewed with his eyes shut ; felt his jaw, and mopped his face, swallowing convulsively with jerks.

And when he was not eating he drank ; lifting his glass and inviting a neighbour to examine those foreign bodies within, which he indicated with all the fervour of a naturalist, and which they saw by the million with the eye of faith.

From the head of the table Clovis-Abel watched with resignation and deep melancholy, knowing he had not the moral stamina to send the boy away. So he waited and refused to see ; hoping that the pudding would provide less of this distasteful hilarity.

But no. When it came it was described with loathsome simile and prodded gingerly as though it were alive ; asleep ; hibernating or recently dead.

And the Frog's own appetite stole away and left him ; they called the pudding : " Donkey-lying-down-in-mud."

But all things end in time. At length there was a sudden rumble and the talking ceased.

William said a Latin grace at speed, and then gave out a notice about the wearing of greatcoats at the match that afternoon, and in so doing split an infinitive. Whereupon Gray and Nigel, those cultured fools, winced. Johnny, whose meal had been interrupted by the general uprising, snatched a last mouthful and hastened out of the hall with a couple of friends, still harping upon his Housemaster's cuisine ; and why not, my dear Frog, since the food is at school an evergreen topic ; as is the weather in England, and *l'estomac* in France.

CHAPTER IX

"Le bonheur consiste simplement à se fermer les yeux ! "—BAUDELAIRE.

LATER in November, William said : " Do you know how stuffy it is in here ? I wonder you can sit in it." And stood twiddling the Common Room door-knob, whilst the inmates glowered at him in sour discomfort, and mourned the departed froust.

"Do please come in or out and shut the door," said Throssell, shrinking away into his chair as a draught like a swirl of icy water cut at his ankles.

So William came in and spread himself before the fire and said he thought it was going to snow.

"Oh, no. I don't think so, I can always tell by the smell," rejoined Warner, who had lived in the Wide, Open Spaces and knew the moods of Nature and the flavours of God's fresh air.

William took a cursory glance round the room, sniffing. " The smell in here is that of station waiting-room-cum-tannery," he said aggressively, " and I didn't know you'd been out this morning."

Warner replied firmly that he had had a free period from 10 till 11, and had been down into the village for tobacco, and that any room was stuffy after a taste of the country-side.

William regretted that his own sense of smell was so poorly developed. He himself had never got beyond the kipper, garlic, acetylene, syringa stage. Those he knew to a T. directly they entered his nostrils.

Then a coal spat and he crossed over to stamp out the sparks upon the carpet.

Cardington, Sixth Form master, stirred in his chair behind his newspaper and ran his fingers through his hair, which though grey was still thick on top, and curly. He recrossed his legs.

Frog began to saw the pages of an uncut book, and Teacher lifted his spectacles on to his forehead and gazed out of the window. It was a flat, bleak day, devoid of colour. The sap no longer rose in the trees, still against an empty sky; and over the country-side was a winter silence.

" It really is too cold for golf, and I think I shall go down to the church and do a little brass-rubbing," said Teacher to no one in particular.

Then he turned to Clovis-Abel and told him he should see the village church, a perfect specimen of Early Perpendicular work. Frog said : " What fun." For he still had very little control over expressions of pleasure and interest.

Teacher was a thought exasperated and went on to explain to Clovis-Abel that near the church stag's antlers had been dug up, which it was thought dated from the time when the Thames was a tributary of the Rhine.

"Ah," said William deeply, "*those* were the days!" and he offered to take them both down to the village in his car, as he was going to the station to fetch books.

"We'd better get off now before it snows," he added, and the three of them went out together.

Warner and Cardington thrust out their empty chairs and drew in closer to the fire.

Warner said he found Dean very trying; but Cardington thought William an excellent fellow who did everybody else's grumbling for them.

Fifteen minutes later the brass-rubbers met William in the courtyard and stamped their feet, looking up at the sky, whilst Simon Kedge rolled back the doors of the Barn and the car was trundled out by hand from a cavernous gloom.

It was as cold as a stone, and Simon took off his coat and set to work with the starting-handle, while Frog and Teacher climbed into the back and sat on the edge of the seat, their eyes half closed, jolted now and then by Kedge's more successful efforts. And William fussed with a hand-throttle and smothered the nascent quivers of the engine with deep stabs upon the accelerator.

Finally they got off, after Kedge had produced a candle-end and warmed the sparking-plugs over its flame.

They bowled down hill, and William flung a lot of conversation over his shoulder, of which Frog and Teacher heard nothing on account of the noise. After a while he realised they were talking French, which was not very polite of them; and

William made allowances for them; the clever fellows probably did not notice which tongue they spoke. Well, it was the thoughts that mattered and not the mode of expression. William hummed a little tune and gazed away over the hedgerows. He was still making allowances for them, when, sweeping lavishly round a bend, he came upon a fleshy pink mound in the road, and had no time to avoid it. He swerved, but passed over it with two soft and horrible bumps, and pulled up five yards on with a scream of brakes.

"Sacred name of a pipe," ejaculated William, "what is it we have overrun now?" and *that* stopped the Gallic chatter in the back seat.

Out they got, much shaken, and there behind upon the road outstretched, was a huge pig, decapitated and immobile.

"How dreadful," said Teacher in hushed tones, "and yet I did not hear it squeal."

William strode away and bent down over it: "You couldn't very well have done. It did its last squeal some days ago in the slaughter-house, poor creature." Then he turned to Clovis-Abel who was shivering and said: "Since many days, pork."

"Whatever shall we do with it? I wonder who it can belong to?" Teacher questioned with an averted face.

William stood thinking. "If it's a local pig," he said, "it must belong to Smith or Frankinson and has dropped off one of their vans. But we haven't time to go round notifying them. No.

We'll drive straight to the police station and they can send up the ambulance or Black Maria or a hearse or whatever they think fit. Or we might leave it at the Almshouses as an early Christmas gift from the school. Or shall I take it home to Mrs. Turvey to pickle for the House Supper ? "

Both Throssell and Clovis-Abel shuddered at these alternatives. And William decided to go to the police station.

" But it can't be left here in the road, poor creature," he said humanely, and fetched the starting handle from the car and levered the gutted corpse into the ditch.

" Should we not cover it over in case of theft ? " ventured Teacher.

" Well," said William testily, repulsion stirring in him at last, " you may give it your greatcoat if you like, but it shall not have mine, or the rug, and the ditch is quite deep enough to hide it from cars, and if a pedestrian cares to carry it away in his arms he may, and I'll never touch pork again as long as I live ! "

He lead the way back to the car.

At the church he dropped his brass-rubbing colleagues, and leaving a vivid message at the police station, went on to the railway station for his books.

There was some hitch over the business, and he had to stand about for over ten minutes, tried beyond endurance by the rattle and clatter of milk-cans and the draughty whistling indolence of the place.

On the way home he came by the main street, and found it up, with ropes and trenches, mounds of earth and broken asphalt, a clump of hurricane lamps, and the rise and fall of pick-axes.

Standing by the wreckage on the untouched strip of road was a sturdy beggar with red flag and muffler ; one of the Idle Poor, and a mill-stone about the nation's neck ; who straightway waved William on from one direction and a dray from the other, and sent them both down a blind alley behind him.

And when William, having extricated himself, was grinding past the Baptist Chapel in bottom gear, he was deceived by hooligans crying out ; and actually stopped in time to hear : " Hi, mister, yer wheels are going round ! "

But the worst was yet to come ; for outside the " King's Arms " he saw a dreadful thing.

Two milk carts were drawn up, one close behind the other, and in the back of the foremost cart was a can with a tap in its side ; and the hindmost horse was licking, *licking*—this dribbling tap !

William gasped and made straight for home in horror and disgust.

When Julia came in he poured it all out to her. She listened, sitting on the fender-stool in the dining-room, and held her hands out to the fire.

At the end she said tranquilly : " Did you notice the name on the cart, William ? Was it our milk ? "

Her husband's heart stood still.

In his emotion he had not done so.

Until this moment he had looked upon the

incident as no more than a glaring example of the government's wanton and shameful negligence in leaving milk in private hands ; but now the affair took on a hideous personal aspect. Appalling visions rose up before him, one after another. He saw the whole House down with diphtheria and typhoid ; his children at death's door, and himself ruined.

Julia was calm. As his news preceded the arrival of the afternoon's milk, every drop could be boiled. She would see Mrs. Turvey at once. She then straightened his collar and tie, the set of which had become Bohemian in his distraction ; and saw Mrs. Turvey, who hearing half the tale, broke in flatly, saying : " Poison. Rank poison." Adding that poison never did good Christians any harm. However, she took no risks with William, who had an early cup of tea before going into school, and with it milk so blue and strong-smelling as to testify to the interval of its separation from the cow.

This was assuredly none of what William had seen dribbling from the can into the horse's mouth ! And Julia hoped he was satisfied.

William took his meal dry and went into school.

Julia meant to write to the dairy, but sat down at the piano and lost herself in Spanish music.

William came out of school at 6 o'clock, still brooding heavily. His heart still grieving over what his eye had seen. He'd had a bad day he said. That was the long and short of it. She now knew the state of the milk and had better be told of the sort of things that happened to the pork and bacon.

Then followed the Story of the Pig ; together with a general summary of the day's grievances, a rehearsal of his woes, the cold, the damp, Warner's attitude in Common Room, the pain and labour of getting the car started, the girlish squeamishness of Throssell and de Mesière over the Pig, his discomfort at the station, the howling mockery of the hooligans, and lastly an illuminating description of that lewd fellow with muffler, his conduct and mentality.

" Don't make heavy weather over trifles, William," said his wife, and picked two flattened currants off the carpet.

Then she sent him upstairs to change, as he was dining with the Headmaster.

If he went up now and dressed early, he would have time to get thoroughly warm and in a sweeter temper before he went out.

Twenty minutes later he re-appeared for Julia to tie his tie ; but she was not in the dining-room, so he went along to his study, and there he found John Fenn sprawling in a chair, sucking an empty pipe, with his feet on the fender. His understudy rose quickly, scattering the fire-irons.

" Don't move, don't move, please," said William, and sat down on a sofa.

From underneath came scratchings, growls and smothered sneezes. William sprang up and lifted the vallance. There in shadow lay Tim ; and with his legs on high, pressed against the springs of William's sofa, he propelled himself, back-scratching, on William's parquet.

H

William hauled him out and handed him over to his master. " You really must control your puppy dog," he said, and Fenn, disconcerted, smacked Tim hard, and turned him out of the French window.

Tim ran away into the night, barking ; warm and glowing after his chastisement.

They sat in silence for a while, then William said : " You don't look very happy, my good man, what is it ? "

John Fenn put away his pipe and looked into the fire.

" I feel cramped, sir," he said, " and I wish I wasn't a schoolmaster. I feel as if I knew exactly what I shall do, every day till my death."

" The old, old story," William said. " But are you a schoolmaster yet ? I think not. Do you remember what Rupert Brooke remarked in them ? : ' That sort of slightly irritated tolerance and lack of irresponsibility.' Well, you haven't got that yet, you see. In fact you're a mere child. You lose your gown ; you forget to pay your washing ; you leave your dog's unspeakable brush and comb about in my study, and you don't even have tidy hair yourself. A schoolmaster ! " William snorted.

John Fenn sat up smiling, his arms round his knees.

" I'm sorry about all those things, sir, and I'll see to them ; but even if I don't yet behave like one, I get the life and duties of a schoolmaster. And it came over me to-day that there's no width in this life, and no change. And because I'm a schoolmaster, my life is now at its highest point ; just because I'm young and up-to-date.

" From now on my life declines. In this profession, it seems to me, you can grow old but not
venerable."

William waved his hand, cutting him short.

" You are a very silly young man," he said. " If
you felt like this, why ever did you come into the
trade ? Chemistry is a live thing. You can make
money by it. You'd better go away and use it in
the wide world. Or go and join your coffee-planting
uncles in Java ; or go round the world before the
mast ; only for pity's sake don't stay here eating
your heart out amongst those resigned to their
fate. There's no need for *you* to die in harness."

William used this harness metaphor when feeling
particularly sorry for himself as a pedagogue ; and
when reminded that he would be pensioned off at
threescore years, he would state that he did not
mean physical death ; but the gradual decease of
his sense of humour and proportion ; and his
realisation of an outside world.

But now, hearing the profession so maligned, he
felt called upon to defend it.

" There is sense in your remarks," he told John
Fenn. " But why have you found out these things
so soon ? I think it must be hearsay, and what
you read. Have you read ' Mr. Perrin and Mr.
Trail ' ? "

Fenn said no.

" Or ' War Among Ladies ' ? "

No. Fenn had not read that either.

" But you shall," said William ; and told him
furthermore that his depression was due to the stage

they had reached in the term. Half-term was well over, but Christmas was yet an immense way off. He would get his second wind in a few days, William told him, and he would get used to school terms again instead of those swift and giddy university affairs ; where you had barely time to open an account at the shops, before you went down again.

" There is truth in what you say," he continued, " about the decline of the profession and the value you have when fresh from the Varsity ; modern ; good at games, perhaps ; and low on the Burnham Scale. Inexpensive. Nice for the Governors. But you take a blinkered view of other trades. You mustn't think of the Church in terms of Bishops and Archbishops ; nor the Stage in Leading Gents or Ladies ; nor the Law in terms of Judges and opulent Divorce-court Barristers.

" And doctoring may not lead to Harley Street. You must take the average man and his chances. Ours is no different from other men's jobs. An ordinary man will make an ordinary schoolmaster, parson, doctor, or whatever he chooses ; and a flabby man will be a flabby one. We're in the same plight as any other sort of breadwinner."

John Fenn mused. " I didn't just drift into this," he said. " I thought it all over. I wanted to teach, and I like that part of it ; but it's this realisation of the narrowness."

" 'Tisn't narrow," answered William bluntly ; " only there's time for introspection. What you need is practical stimulus ; something beside reading ; talk with other men ; not just laying down

the law by turn, as we get in Common Room.
And the effect of a stream of boys coming and
growing up and going, makes you feel stationary.
But, my good Fenn, you've not given this a fair
trial. And you mustn't judge from my House,
which is rather turbulent. But I don't apologise
for it. Oh, no! I rather like it. I quite like it.
But if you leave, and mark you, I'm not pressing
you, just leave before you become a comfort to me.
But it's too late. You already take preparation
quite faultlessly and carve very nicely as well.
Besides I'm stiffening up; my caning is not what
it was. Suppose you stay. And now I must go.
Mind you put the fireguard on if you leave the
room; and I won't have your tripehound in here,
mouthing the upholstery."

In the drawing room William caught Julia, who
tied his tie.

Miss Greig was there as well, asking him if there
was anything in the paper to-day; a funny question,
thought William, from one who was neither blind
nor paralysed.

And then down came the nursery governess with
the news that Andrew would not say his prayers.
What a day! A procession of calamities. And
now he must cope with his first-born. Eventually
he got off to his dinner party, and returned refreshed,
for the Headmaster had a pretty taste in claret;
and he was moreover the one person who did not
excite William's rhetorical grumblings.

With him, William was at rest; for in his company he lost that sense of petty haste and festering

trivialities, and no longer felt himself bucketing down to the grave ' with his future behind him.' Wrinkles were smoothed from his brow. With the Headmaster his brain was unflurried ; there was peace and well-being and time to think ; and thoughts worth thinking came to him. His heart beat steadily, and there, or so it seemed to him, the very ticking of the clocks was less hurried than elsewhere ; and time paused. It was a lull in his life. And then he came home, and as he returned his troubles crowded in upon him.

For he could not, like Walpole, throw off his worries as he threw off his clothes ; and so got into bed encumbered with personal grievances, domestic uncertainties, national anxieties, international alarms, and universal perplexities ; and he lay there staring at the cracks in the ceiling, and worrying as to where the milk came from ; where the drains went to ; the Labour Party ; the next Budget ; Disarmament ; Relativity and the Lord knows what ; and finally dropped off to sleep with the light on ; and when he awoke in the morning, it was still keeping a sickly vigil above his head, what time the light of another common day was coming in through the window.

CHAPTER X

"The day was still-born."
— MASEFIELD.

DECEMBER came with rains and mist hiding the fields. And dawn was one with twilight, cold and silent, blind and smothered in the fog.

A pale drenched dawn, with sodden turf and raindrops gleaming on the twigs. The Headmaster meant to catch the London train, but missed it and came crawling home with feeble yellow headlights, and his chauffeur crimson-nosed and furious at missing a day off in the village; for as the Proprietor was a bachelor, there was no wife expecting the car back on these occasions.

When he got home again the Headmaster asked for the breakfast coffee to be re-heated. Then he had a boy out of school and beat him hard for everything in general. After which he sent off an order for Christmas cards; wrote to an Old Boy in Vienna; finished his notes for the Headmasters' Conference; read *The Times'* fourth Leader; and then sent for his secretary and delivered another instalment of a correspondence with the Governors over the expense of certain bathrooms in Throssell's

House, now in process of construction, and known to the School as " Teacher's Marble Halls."

At noon the porter tolled the bell in the quadrangle ; and the place became black with boys, uncertain in the fog.

Nigel came down from the Library and hunted for Gray.   No one had seen him.

When Nigel got back to William's House he found that Gray was in the Sick-room.   It was mild influenza, Polly said, and went on to say that Gray was asking for his books, so that he might work in bed.

" A likely tale ! " thought Nigel, and after dinner he crossed off their names for a fives court and went for a run instead.

He slipped off quietly into the mist, taking a bridle path over the high ground to the North, in the opposite direction to the village.

He ran over a great bare field, curving away into the fog, a rich stretch of plough-land, and red ; unlike the soil round his home.

And here the mist was thin, but below on all sides of the field it rolled, impenetrable and white as clouds about a mountain, giving a sense of loneliness upon a height ; and save for his footsteps, regular and light, and his breathing, there was a dead silence and the bitter smell of fog.

Leaving the path he dipped into a copse, with the mist hanging chill about the tree-boles and the ground slippery with leaves ; and then out into the open, skirting a pleached hedge for a quarter of a mile.

His breath was like smoke; he was warm and wet. He sprinted to a gate and a button came off his shirt.

He passed a cottage with no sign of life, and the rain chuckling into a green water-butt.

It had a tumbledown thatch of straw; a poor thing, he considered, when compared with the reed-thatching in his own country.

He passed another cottage, and children on the door-step, with yellow curls and dirty mouths, who stared.

Then he came to a road and ran for a mile in and out of ruts, between loose stone walls.

Here he met cart-horses, clopping slowly through the mud, huge in the mist, one dappled and one black. And carters sitting sideways, whistling, lazy and uncaring in the rain, with sacks round their shoulders, and boots shapeless with mud. One was wearing out his Sunday trousers; they were purple as pickled cabbage, and his black horse steamed.

" Where be yew going to so fast ? " they cried; and Nigel turned his head and hollered that he was running away from school. Whereat they chuckled and spat and spoke to their horses. And the fog swallowed them; but their voices still came to him, an idle mumble.

After that Nigel slowed down and made round in a circle back towards the school, running beside a young larch wood and through two farmyards. Joining the main road, he fell in with a drove of junior boys; panting, with rain-flattened hair;

running with high chins, clenching their fists. They opened out to let him pass; and cars went by slowly bleating in the fog.

Farther on he overtook mixed infants, trotting in a string home from school, with cherry noses, and the mist glistening in their hair.

Round the next bend he came upon and slipped between a couple of huge old women with bundles of washing beneath their arms, muffled to the eyes, and up top their husbands' tweed " gorblimey " caps; and he left them far behind.

As he approached the main school buildings the Chapel clock struck four, measurely. The mist had thinned, and already there were lights about the place; not the snug orange lights of private houses, but lights diffused in halls and corridors and class-rooms.

Nigel had a bath on arrival; after which he went to see William about the House Play, and passed through double doors into the carpeted silence of the private house.

William was in his study, with the cat before the fire, and papers upon his knee.

The cat rose, stretched, crisping her claws, and walked sinuously round and about Nigel's legs, in a figure of eight. Nigel scratched her behind the ears and she arched her neck with a sonorous purr.

" Ah ! " said William, " it's you, is it ?   Sit down and wait.   I'm adding up a column."

He put his fingers to his ears and his lips moved silently as if in prayer.

Nigel lowered himself on to the sofa.

" You look at last night's Parliamentary Report," William advised, giving him *The Times*, " fur flew last night. They're getting very catty in the House, I'm afraid. They spend their time wrangling inconclusively, while the Nation slowly strangles." And he said it was only another case of the incurable imbecility of human nature.

When he had finished his accounts, they began to talk of the House Play.

The committee had met a week ago ; a play had been chosen and parts allotted, to be learnt during the holidays. For the School House and three others gave performances at Christmas, and William and the rest at the end of the Lent Term.

At the close of the meeting William had said that although the play chosen was not a masterpiece of English Drama, and polished mummers few and far between in the House, he had, as ever, confidence in his Leading Ladies. They, with their contralto charms, would, he knew, lift the play on to the level of other performances given in past years. For in William's House it was traditional that Leading Ladies should be on an heroic scale, with policemen's feet and hands like bunches of bananas.

This struck a welcome contrast with those shrill milk-and-water fledgelings presented by other Houses.

Now, as the Play was short, the committee had decided upon three ten-minute intervals with music.

But William had made inquiries.

There were, he discovered, but four musicians in

the House, and none of them any credit to St. Cecilia.

A couple of squealing fifes he had found, together with a puce-visaged flautist, and one who learnt, but did not play, the violin.

The Big Drum was also in the House; 6 ft. 3 in., with arms like flails. And William scouted the committee's suggestion that these should make music together, banked in with evergreen boscage beside the stage.

Ear-ravagers, he said they were, one and all (hearing them flogging up " Marche Militaire "), and he spoke of the double sweetness of the unheard melody.

And as each of the other Houses had an orchestra, it was felt there could be no stooping from hand-made music to a gramophone; nor did William offer the services of Polly, or his wife, to sing and play, as had been hoped. So there was to be a Curtain Raiser. This was William's idea to fill in the time, and Nigel had at once offered three, written by himself during recent years; and William had asked for them, and had taken away the manuscripts to read.

Number one was called " The Three Unities," and took three minutes to act. There were many stage-directions. The scene was a " chambre à volonté." In the middle distance stood one Boileau, belching forth instructions, and in his hand a wee egg-glass with swiftly trickling sand.

Under Boileau's nose, to William's surprise, stood Corneille, Molière and Racine, shivering in a cluster;

and about them surged the creatures of their brains.

In dumb show at their elbow, Titus, Rubens-limbed, took leave of Berenice, with rapid hesitations. The air was charged with moral victories and defeats ; heavy with the recital of woes, and the stage shook with the chronic arrival of messengers. To one side, the brothers Horace and Curiace with wives and sisters, stood apart in their symmetrical dilemma.

From behind them a man called Rodrigue bawled out the tale of a sea-fight. All Confidantes silted up together in the wings, a timid bevy ; whilst encircling the whole troupe was a ' chaîne d'amants ' hand in hand, despairing ; A in love with B, and B with C, and C with D, and so on, *ad infinitum.*

The piece was dedicated to Clovis-Abel de Mesière, but that had been scratched out.

The second curtain-raiser, called " That Way Madness Lies," smacked both of Vaudeville and Pantomime, and dealt with the quainter forms of lunacy.

Its Principal Boy was a monumental mason who was convinced that he was Michelangelo.

And a chorus had come into being suddenly, three years ago, when Nigel, reading Pope, had found :

" Here living teapots stand, one arm held out,
  One bent ; the handle this, and this the spout."

And there was a happy ending, for they died, the loons, and went to Their Own Place, which was neither Heaven nor Hell, but the Moon. And they had it all to themselves too, except for St. Francis, who lived alone in a valley.

And the monumental mason sat there in a white light, and heard the music of the spheres, and chipped at shining marble. And round about the moon the eternal space was blue ; and far below he saw the Earth, a bustling sphere, toiling and seething. . . .

And Nigel's third curtain-raiser was a scandalous affair called " The Murder of Shakespeare."

The scene was laid in Shakespeare's house, where his servants flew about his kitchen and spoke to one another in their master's phrases. Thus, for instance, an under-scullion, a lily-livered boy, appearing from Shakespeare's larder with finger to nose and an averted face, would wail as he swung a putrefying fowl :

" That it should come to this. But two months dead !
　Nay, not so much, not two."

And William, reading this, was horrified and found it blasphemous, and gave it back to Nigel hoping that it would reach the waste-paper basket before shocking anyone else. It was not a thing for squeamish minds, he said.

Nigel crushed it into a ball and threw it on the fire, where it expanded, turning brown, and caught alight with a plop. The cat opened her eyes at the flame, and the scorched paper blackened ; the writing stood out and disappeared. Charred scraps went up the chimney, and the rest hung on the coals, quivering, pale, and as light as foam.

And William said that he must re-write the moon-crazy one, to be read ; to be conceived in the mind, but not acted.

Something might be made of " The Three Unities," William thought, but not as a preface to a House Play, and certainly not to this House Play.

" I'm thankful to see though," he added, " that you've not been tinkering with Phèdre. She was on a grand scale, and her miseries upset me quite as much as Lear's and Hamlet's and Othello's.

" She and that green-ribboned misanthrope are the only ones I care about in the whole crew."

And he was going on about Phèdre's miseries, when the door opened and Mrs. Turvey swirled in upon them.

She folded her hands, glared, and said he ought to know that there were Waits outside in the court-yard, singing their heads off in the fog ; beautiful Christian tunes, and what was he going to give them ?

William said he thought she knew he never gave a penny before the end of term, and expressed him-self on these little Yuletide beasts who come cater-wauling beneath the windows, before the leaves are off the trees. But Mrs. Turvey lifted up her voice and carried on the argument.

Such a voice it was ! A loud, lugubrious drone, like the wind on a stormy night ; and like the wind it would rise to a squall, and there were lulls too, for the asthmatic intake of breath.

And William thought of all the things that upset him most, like dead matches, lumps in porridge, and The Governors, and decided that Mrs. Turvey's voice came before any of these things.

Until he met her he had always thought of Helen of Troy and Mary Queen of Scots as the most troublesome and havoc-making women in the world; but now Mrs. Turvey was added to the list, and he put her first.

Then Julia came in and Mrs. Turvey went away, taking the cat with her.

" I came down to fetch you, William," Julia said. " They've nearly finished tea—and it's Andrew's birthday," she explained to Nigel.

" Ah, now," said William, " I thought it didn't feel like an ordinary day. You'd better come along and pull a cracker too, if you've time."

And so Nigel followed them upstairs and through twisty passages towards the nursery.

On the way there William asked what he had been doing that afternoon; and Nigel said he'd been for a run over the North Ridge and home by the farms.

" Ah," said William, " you want to know the country in this weather. I'm told that Mr. Warner's children went out this morning with their governess and got lost in the lanes, and turned up at two o'clock this afternoon in the baker's van."

Then at the end of the passage was the nursery door, with a line of brightness below, and voices.

Julia opened the door and Nigel bent his head to enter, and went down two steps on to green linoleum.

They were all hard at it still, eating in paper hats, the children ; about ten of them. The bulk belonging to other masters ; and at the head of the table Andrew, sticky and spoilt among his presents.

The litter was shifted, and his parents discovered their clean plates and sat down.

The nurse filled up a little brown tea-pot and gave Nigel a mug. He drank down his tea and found a teddy-bear grinning at him on the bottom. All round him other people's children ate, and drank great draughts of milk, and began to blow upon the whistles from their crackers.

Nigel found a seat at a corner of the table beside Peter Dean, who was drinking milk steadily with both hands to his mug, his saucer eyes fixed upon his brother's birthday cake and its nine candles ; and on the other side of him sat Warner's youngest daughter, who had been lost that morning in the fog.

A Botticelli child she was, with thin fingers, and she asked Nigel to take the sting out of her cracker, and to tie on the false nose they found inside. This he did, knotting the strings behind her head. And she told him all about the ride home in the baker's van. She sat on a sack, she said, speaking slowly, and it was warm and dusky, and a lovely smell of new bread, and she had listened to the horse's hoofs and nearly went to sleep.

Then Andrew hailed him from the head of the table, and gave him a piece of his cake, cutting from the shorter wall of the gap in it. Nigel

I

picked the silver balls off the sugar and saved them till the last. William's nursery was a pleasant room, long and low like his study ; with cupboards and a spotted rocking-horse, blue curtains, high fireguard, and cocks and hens and what not trotting round upon a frieze.

By and by William pushed back his chair, and with his hands made rabbit-shadows on the wall. After this the party began collecting gelatine paper from the crackers and smoothing it out.

William sat still in reverie. He was pleased.

For soon the term would end, and all those feet and voices would take themselves off to their own homes ; and life would cease for a time to be divided up by bells. There would be a little golf with Julia's brothers during the day, and at night a little Bridge without Miss Greig. And large fires and devilled bones for breakfast, and time to eat them ; and above all, the worst noises in the world would cease.

The worst noises in the world were Phonetics, servants' laughter and ' chopsticks ' on the dining-hall piano.

For when William caught the sound of Phonetics in a neighbouring classroom he winced, and it was to his ear as the squeak of raw cabbage leaves, or the rasp of a knife's edge upon a plate. And often he would talk to Clovis-Abel of these things. And servants' laughter—those gusts of mirth which came to him when the kitchen door swung open, strident and sustained—they too would die away, for the main body of the servants departed for the holidays.

And Heaven alone knew what they found to laugh about. As for 'chopsticks,' next term he would forbid them altogether ; for wherever he was in the House, through windows and down corridors, this hell-bred jangle reached him !

Any more of it, and he would have in the dumb piano from the Barn !

But with this blessed and approaching peace, there was no need further to excite himself. It was now the first week in December, and to-morrow would see the beginning of the end ; for carols would be sung in Chapel, unhymnlike, quaint, with old inconsequent words—echoes of a time when joys were simple things and sorrows deep and simple, and sins black and distinct, uninvolved with subconscious influences and complexes.

So William pondered on those times. He often did ; and when pinned down to say what period it was he meant, and advised by Warner to consider the dirt, cold, smell and insecurity of the Mediæval Age, he would answer that what he had in mind was no particular epoch, but an atmosphere, an inter-mittent flavour of the past, childlike and irretriev-able, a twinkling sincerity, present in those Carols and in Nativity Plays, on Pageant Carts, with Herod so cramped, permitted to get down and rave ; and brightly shown in Chaucer, who had a merry eye ; and known, this spirit—the ancient wisdom of a child, unselfconscious, shining—to Ronsard and du Bellay ; sweetly copied by Spenser ; strong in Shakespeare ; waning after him ; unknown to the Romantics, whose vision was not childlike, but adolescent. And this spirit, he felt sure, was thwarted by the Industrial Revolution—root of all evil in William's eyes—stealing individuality and turning simple people off the land, their natural home. But he fancied he saw it again in Bernard Shaw's "Saint Joan," and knew he did in Bridges's "Testament of Beauty."

And certain of those young poets dying in the War; they knew it and took it with them to their graves.

So then Carols would be sung to-morrow; first sign of the term's ending. And he would listen, hunched in his gown. The hours William had sat listening to one thing and another, hunched in his gown! Singing, sermons and lessons in Chapel; orders, advice and argument in Common Room; lectures and recitals in Big School, when strange men and women sang and played, high and low, loud and soft; wood-wind, brass-wind, pianoforte, strings—the whole gamut!

And politicians came, and statesmen came, and bronzed explorers too. And William sat in his gown in high detachment, similar to that of the statuary around the walls—those marble Greeks and Romans. For whatever was said or sung, they stood apart in a remote white loveliness. And William, sitting through these entertainments, found comfort in their unchanging faces.

Slowly he brought his mind to bear on present things, recalled to his nursery and Andrew's birthday by a general 'getting down' of the company; the untying of feeders and a mutter of "Thank

God for my good tea." Down the stairs he went
again with Nigel, who was thanking him, and who
went away with the manuscript of the rejected
Curtain-raisers, to work, he said.

But Nigel, reaching his study, put off his work,
and lay back in his chair, regretting that he was
no longer a child to mewl and puke at will; to sit
and bite his toes before a nursery fire; to gurgle
with legs at an angle of 90 degrees to the body,
and creases of fat like bracelets at the wrist. And
he should like Andrew's age over again, when
thoughts were still half-feelings.

And he'd had a prime early youth himself, for
which he gave thanks, remembering the countless
jam-spoons he had licked and the uproarious baths
he'd had in his time, sousing the nurse and setting
the other children crying and howling. And then
right back in the distance he could remember
riding in his pram, a great high pram, in the sun;
when he would shout and toss his bonnet over-
board, and look down, clutching the sides, to watch
the uncovered wheels going round below, with
flattened leaves and little stones and bits of muck
reappearing regularly upon the tyres. And now,
whenever he saw a baby in its pram, he was gnawed
by an emerald jealousy, thinking: " If it's two
now, then when it's twenty I shall be nigh on
forty, thin on the temples and in a flap about my
first varicose vein!" He had once spoken to
William about this shocking passage of time; the
way it whirled you on with each tick of the
clock.

133

And William had agreed, saying that he himself had been whisked through his youth all unawares, and now was being carried fussing down towards senility; but that he was counting upon this life being only the rough copy, so to speak, and that he would be given time to get it all straight later on; adding that in consideration of this early hurry and mismanagement, he was expecting a sunny old age, and then he had rounded off this optimism by saying that things were never as bad as they seemed, except when they were worse.

Nigel shook himself, stopped thinking about William, and began to write an essay for Cardington upon the Rights of Man.

And Gray in the sick-room stirred in his sleep.

And John Fenn in the dining hall taking Preparation decided to go on being a schoolmaster.

And Johnny, also in the dining hall, sought to do a sum for William with tolerable honesty, knowing the answer already.

And Andrew in the nursery thought he felt sick.

And Mrs. Turvey in the kitchen thought about nothing whatever, and trod on the cat.

And William in his study thought of Christmas presents; John Fenn should have " Mr. Perrin and Mr. Trail " from himself, whilst Julia should give him " War Among Ladies."

After that William got up and stretched and caught his grandfather's eye above the mantelpiece. A little dim, he thought. He would have the portrait cleaned during the holidays.

Ah, the holidays! They really were in sight. He looked at the calendar; there was only the final of the House matches to be played, and those House Plays to be seen; a recital of Schubert's songs by a friend of Julia's; sermon by the Headmaster; and the Breaking-up Concert, so loud and thankful.

Yes, indeed. The end was not far off!

INTERLUDE

CHAPTER XI

"Le silence illimitible des champs . . . un silence
tranquil, pénétrant et large jusqu'aux astres."
—DE MAUPASSANT.

ON the first night of the holidays Johnny took
a bath, a superb bath, breast-high, with
clouds of steam; and in it he whistled and
sang.

His heart was light and he was deeply thankful,
for he had escaped from mathematics and was
back in his own country again.

Therefore he sang and soaped his toes and lay
back gazing at his knuckles, just above the water-
line, as red as cherries in the heat.

The bath-room was right at the top of the house,
an attic, transformed. It lay between two box-
rooms, and the sounds of the house did not reach
there. It also served as a dark-room, for they took
many photographs and Mark would have these all
developed in the house. So there were extra blinds
and shutters, and high up a shelf of rinsing-pans,
pots, bottles, beakers, drainers—all obscured by the
steam.

After a while, Johnny pulled out the plug and
put his heel above the hole to feel the suck of the

water ; and his heel was drawn into the mouth of the pipe with a jerk.

This he did several times, and as the water ran away gurgling his limbs grew heavier.

He climbed out and sat on the edge of the bath to dry himself ; and now and then paused, one arm out-flung, and hand on heart, trolling like a Prima Donna.

Bathrooms were rare spots for song-effects, he found ; also for instrumental music. Lavender practised her 'cello there—it gave such a tone to the thing ; and far away up in the bath-room its dronings were scarce heard in the house below.

When he was dry Johnny took up his candle and went down to his bedroom, and in the bed was a hot-water bottle in a pink flannel bag with shoulder-straps, and he was very pleased to find it there.

For he had suffered from chilly feet day and night during the latter half of term, and towards the end had never been warm except for an hour or two after games.

Breakfast-time had been the worst, in that immense dining hall with its recently-lit fires, cracking palely in the distance ; draughts striking at his neck ; his cuffs grazing his cold wrists, and the porridge-spoon frozen in his hand. A pretty beginning to the day !

He snorted at these things and snuggled into bed. He did like a bit of comfort. Always had. And cosiness, too. Small rooms, low ceilings and curtains in the window. Those halls and open dormitories ! Might as well sleep out on the Steppes of Russia !

Comfortless they were as the Stable at Bethlehem in Italian pictures, depicted high and vast, with chilly pillars. He just didn't like to think of the draughts there must have been there !

But now he troubled less over that since Mark had told him that these open-work stables were all wrong ; and that it had been a good deep cave ; very probably less draughty than the Inn itself.

Having warmed his toes, Johnny brought up the hot-water bottle and laid it against his stomach. Then he looked round the room, as always last thing, to locate his most precious possessions in case of fire, when he might be too dazed to think out where they were ; and feeling a sneeze gather within him, used it to extinguish his candle.

The night was mild, with stars, and he lay awake a little listening to the stillness.

After a time an owl hooted, and far away a dog began to bark. . . .

There was rain during the night, but it ceased towards morning, and when he woke early and stood before the window, the air came in upon him in its fragrance, cool and fresh as a drink of water.

The sky was rain-washed ; a faint translucent yellow, brightening to gold ; and birds winging slowly across it.

And there were elms beside the house, a rare thing in that country ; feathery, their branches woven on the sky, and rooks cawing about their nests—those untidy blobs, black and matted in the tree-tops. Johnny had a wish to take a rake and comb out every one of them.

Then he remembered that Tim was in the house, and Fenn, too, who had returned with them for Christmas. Johnny went down to the kitchen and found the terrier in his temporary nest, a laundry basket, for he had not been put with their own Cocker and Cairn in the stable.

Tim was awake, bright-eyed and licking softly. At once his bouquet of a tail began to wag. Johnny gathered him, supple and warm, into his arms and made off upstairs with him.

Tim got on to the bed and Johnny into it, humping up his knees, and Timmy climbed about, biting and growling, and went down upon his elbows like a camel, and trundled along rubbing his graceless chaps amongst the blankets, and shook his head, sneezing.

All of a sudden there came a knocking at the door. Timmy paused with his ears inside out and his back legs trailing out behind upon the counterpane.

" Come in," said Johnny, and in came John Fenn in his dressing-gown.

" I thought I heard him," he said grimly, for he slept next door. Timmy slithered off the bed, skidding over the floor toward him, and jumped up at the cords of his dressing-gown, licking and singing.

" You know I never allow him upstairs. And on a bed too ! " said Fenn. " Did he come up here on his own ? "

"No," said Johnny; "I fetched him."

"Well, you ought to know better, with dogs of your own," answered Fenn crisply, and took Timmy away with him, shutting the door.

Johnny flounced down in bed in a tantrum. He was sore, and rehearsed all the things he might have said back to Fenn.

He could have told him that he didn't count his dog as a dog at all, and only thought of him as the sort of thing you saw in a toy-shop, on a green wooden stand.

Besides, it was all very well for the man Fenn to lay down haughty rules for the dog's conduct, when it was obvious how badly brought up it was. He had no control over it.

Why, it was common knowledge that upon Guy Fawkes' Day one of William's socks had been found in its kennel, together with a paper tract on the Gospel of St. Matthew.

And they said, too, that once Fenn had plucked him in the courtyard and that the wind had changed, blowing Tim's superfluous hairs into the kitchens, all over everything.

And had he not himself that day pointed out Tim's whiskers sprouting in the Apple Charlotte?

The clocks began striking eight, and there was another knock at the door.

John Fenn came in again, fully dressed, twirling a muffler.

He was taking Tim out for a run, he said, and would Johnny like to come too?

Johnny accepted gravely and without any of that vulgar enthusiasm. He then tore his way into his clothes, and they went down the back-stairs together and out into the morning; Timmy with no collar, and frisking; and came back with an enormous appetite for breakfast.

CHAPTER XII

" . . . I am a feather for each wind that blows.
Shall I live on ? "
—" *A Winter's Tale.*"
" I do believe her though I know she lies."
—" *The Passionate Pilgrim.*"

FENN had travelled down the day before with Nigel and Johnny, and Tim in the van.

Hour upon hour they journeyed, quitting the main host in London at noon. And about tea-time in an uncertain light, the train drew up at a windy little halt upon a hill, with one porter, one milk can, and a shelter no bigger than a sentry box.

Johnny and Nigel leaned far out of the window, their hair on end.

There was a girl waiting on the platform, and she waved as they swept past. It so happened that their carriage was close behind the engine, and when the train drew up, they were beyond the platform altogether.

Johnny immediately opened the door and dropped down on to the siding that ran parallel to the single track. He waved his arms, shouting, and bawled to the porter by name. And the porter bawled back at him to come on off that there line.

And all along the train heads shot out, thinking there had been an accident.

After a lot of liver-jerking motion the train drew up again ; this time their carriage was level with the sentry box.

Altogether they arrived in style.

The girl came towards them laughing ; her voice was Johnny's, and Nigel introduced her as his sister Lavender. In the dusk Fenn saw nothing of her face.

They trooped along to the van, and Timmy, with a label round his neck, was released, singing and wriggling in an ecstasy of reunion.

Then out came their trunks, which they left to be brought on by carrier's cart, and they followed the sister down wooden steps to the road below. Here there was a car.

Between them they carried their suit-cases, and Nigel and John Fenn had golf-clubs as well. The porter followed behind, empty-handed, to tuck them up safe, as he said.

" Goo you on, 'bor," said Johnny, rallying him, " you'll catch cold wait'n for remuneration." And he went on with badinage to inquire after the porter's nose—*proboscis gules*, he called it ; but the man, a huge, black-eyed creature, slow and mellow, understood nothing of the euphemism, and mumbled and grinned as he strapped the suit-cases on behind.

Finally all was stowed away ; Johnny, Timmy, Lavender and the golf-clubs in the back of the car beneath rugs ; and Nigel driving, with John Fenn beside him.

"Be you all right together?" asked the porter, and Nigel clapped a florin into his palm.

They said they were, wishing him good night, God-speed, a Merry Christmas, a Happy New Year, and countless other blessings.

He gave a shrill whistle between his fingers, and away they went down a dark road between pine trees; and the wind in these sounded like the sea.

They reached the house in twenty minutes; came up a rise to it, hooting lustily, and flowed in upon a man who said he'd never heard such a noise, and shook Fenn's hand, and asked after his mother.

And by the lamplight John Fenn took a look at the sister.

She was slim, with a long throat and Nigel's eyes.

Johnny had greenish eyes, brilliant; but Nigel's and the sister's were grey with a look of distance in them; the look Miss Greig always said she saw in the eyes of airmen and sailors! And the sister's hair was dark, pushed away from her face, and she had a long Rossetti line from the ear-lobe to the point of the chin, and thin wrists like a child.

She was, he knew, just a year younger than Nigel, and like her brothers she stood and moved with a straight grace, natural and rare, and not to be confused with that "head up and shoulders back" deportment instilled by physical culture.

Usually she spoke with Johnny's intonation; but at dinner she asked after William, quoting a few of his phrases in a voice which was quite a good imitation of Nigel's imitation of William's voice.

And she asked also after " Teacher " and " Frog," and whether Penhurst was still as old for his years ; and how Nigel and Gray had enjoyed being prefects, and whether Johnny liked fagging for Gray, and how Rat Day had gone off ?

In fact, there was really nothing she did not touch upon. All those questions she had refrained from asking on paper during the term, came out now in a rush, and her eyes shone at having them at home again.

But her brothers did not expand, and were non-committal in reply.

John Fenn was amused at their almost unconscious resentment of her chatter. It bored them, and he felt that they did not like it said before him. After all he was a master. Perhaps the sister did not think of him as one, as he had only been there one term. Maybe she considered him only as the son of her father's friend. But then she turned to him and asked him how he liked being a schoolmaster ; and whether it was a very narrow life. John Fenn, remembering William's discourse, said briefly that he was getting used to it, and went no further into the question. He thought over Nigel and Johnny's displeasure and decided that it came from the fact that it was unnatural in a sister to know so much of the everyday goings-on of school life. Of course it was quite in order that sisters should take an interest in these affairs ; but it went down better, Fenn opined, if it was an old-fashioned, wide-eyed, simple feminine interest ; with a fondly-foolish idea to be set right here, and a quaintly-foolish question to be answered there.

He decided also that this sister's peculiar interest came from pure affection and from insufficient home-interests. Of course, it must be that.

He asked her how long ago she had left school herself? She told him, only just last summer, and that she was going to Paris next Easter. She had not gone before because she had had 'flu in her last term at school. Besides, she said, her father wanted to get used to being childless gradually. For Johnny's Prep. school was in the neighbourhood, and they had seen him frequently. But now of course it was different, with both of them away.

In Paris she would go on with her 'cello. John Fenn explained to her the whereabouts of his mother's Flat there, and then talked of the bookstalls down by the Seine, and how you could no longer get at the books to look at them.

Lavender said that she must go there at Easter and see what she could find.

Next morning, when Fenn came in from exercising Tim, he found Dr. Bentley standing before the fire, eating his porridge and reading his sons' school reports.

He found them uninteresting, he said.

Johnny's was non-committal throughout, and Nigel's naked and scanty. But he realised that Sixth Form work was so rare and specialised that there could be very little to say about it that a parent could understand.

And Mark regretted their Prep. school reports. He had always enjoyed those, so full and chatty, with prophecies as to a rosy future; like an interview with a gipsy.

But he was glad to see that Dean found their conduct satisfactory.

"Satisfactory am I?" said Nigel indignantly. "Nothing more than that? When I was expecting 'Has been of invaluable assistance'; or 'Has proved himself a tower of strength'; or 'Has served the House ungrudgingly throughout the term.' From 'satisfactory' you might never guess the way I wrote out lists, helped pudding, carved joints and went round shutting windows at night; toiling fit to break my back!"

Then catching Fenn's eye he added: "But we don't work for reward in this world, do we, sir? No. Let me see, what is it we work for?"

Mark said he didn't think modern youth worked for anything at all.

"Now, now," said Lavender, "no more of that."

"I'm only repeating what your Aunt says."

"What does she say this year?"

Mark began to read.

This was an Aunt who lived in the Highlands. Every year from her bleak home her Christmas letter came, a little previous to the Feast itself, out of consideration to the Postmaster-General; a message to her brother's family; a summing up of the year, and of what it had meant to her and

150

what it should mean to them. Last year's theme
had been " Unemployment," and the year before
that "Free Trade." This year's deductions were
based upon Youth's Outlook. She was not, she
said, one of those creatures who quarrelled with
their outward limbs and flourishes, and wrote to *The
Mirror* signing themselves " Disgusted "; " Maida
Vale," or some such thing. But she did think,
and she held to it, that young people nowadays,
and she stuck to that phrase, were too much inclined to put off doing things.

They put off getting up in the morning; and put
off going to bed at night.

The young men put off earning their living,
and the young women put off having children,
and put off growing old.

Then Aunt went on to talk of grit.

Grit, she said, was more valued in these days
as a quality than it was when she was young;
for then it had been taken for granted.

Mark paused in his reading to let this sink
in.

All bent humbly over their eggs and bacon.

But Johnny hauled toast from the rack, shrilled
out with a crinkled nose that he thought the Old
Bird was quite right. That was just the line he
would be taking with *his* children.

And Mark also supported her with illustrations
from his own youth.

Nigel said : " I should like William to meet my
Aunt ! "

After breakfast they loosed the dogs, went over

the lawns together and down through the kitchen garden to the orchard.

Below the orchard lay the river, pale and shining in the sun. Down there, too, was a boat-house, and a spring-board, telling of summer.

In the orchard they found the wooden cradle for 'slip catches' that Mark had bought years ago, when some preparatory school in the district went bankrupt, withered by the prosperity of Johnny's establishment.

All the autumn this cradle had been full of windfalls. They tossed out a rotten apple, a few leaves and twigs, and between them hoisted it up through the kitchen garden and on to the lawn; a slow business.

Then Johnny fetched a cricket ball and the four of them stood round and threw the ball into the cradle, and out it flew at wizard angles. The dogs ran about barking, and Lavender was in delight.

She had been at this for years. She threw well, and her catching was scarce inferior to that of her brothers. Whenever balls were brought out she brightened and was in her element, enjoying the admiration given her for her straight eye and nimble pair of hands.

In the afternoon they went and rode a farmer's horses, indifferent beasts, a job lot.

And Johnny was given the one the farmer let out for funerals; a scraggy sable rouncy with a jovial eye, and it bolted with him, and he was very much ashamed.

Next day they went in by car to the County

Town to finish their Christmas shopping. Johnny's choice was supervised, for otherwise, as Lavender explained to Fenn, you never knew what he mightn't spring upon you.

Christmas came and went; and John Fenn unwrapped " Mr. Perrin and Mr. Trail " from William, and " War Among Ladies " from Julia, and read them both and pondered.

On Boxing Day they got up early and walked four miles to a Meet. In time they reached the road through the pine wood. The air was sharp and fragrant and the grass to the roadside pale with frost. It was a close wood, a host of trees, and each one straight and like its brother.

The sun was low, and as they walked it went along beside them and winked between the pines, shining so cold.

And Nigel began to talk to John Fenn about some book that had recently been published.

Lavender joined in.

She seemed, thought Fenn, to know a lot about it; and they talked of other books, and she knew about them too.

She disparaged and praised with an eager fluency, that took all colour from the works themselves.

Her vocabulary was unusual but monotonous. Lavender was indeed widely read. In fact the number of books she'd read so as to have them at her fingers' ends for reference and conversation, was astounding.

But when she read, and her polished, smattery criticisms took shape, she would become rapt;

suddenly appreciating the outlook of a poet. And then she desired to have that outlook, and to live for the things for which they lived.

But the world must know that she saw things in this True Light, and renounced Mammon's worthless superficialities. It was not in her to make that renunciation a private matter between herself and her better self.

Lavender had a wide circle of acquaintances, young and uproarious. They followed Mammon. They gave picnics under the moon, and drove great distances in their parents' motor-cars, and danced with mistletoe kisses to follow, and went to race-meetings and backed the wrong horses with inside information, and swore, and were more at home in other people's houses than under the paternal roof. So was Lavender.

On first acquaintance she sparkled and shone ; and if her family were absent, could draw upon the whole stock of their wit and sayings, as she pointed out.

But it was upon first and second sight that she was at her best.

After that something palled. The girl fell between two stools. The quips and jests, though good, were served up in a phraseology that somehow oppressed her contemporaries. Knowledge and information loomed in her presence, and came along with her to dances ; unobtrusive but definitely present.

And Lavender loved dancing, and when not gazing from the poet's outlook at things in their True Light, wondered unhappily why her programme was not as full as some. It was not as though she was hideous, or badly-dressed, or got under people's feet.

And then besides her contemporaries, there were her father's friends, men of solid intellect; men who, if they did use a Greek quotation, used it as naturally as they would their handkerchiefs. They smiled with a lenient contempt for these false-backed goods in Lavender's shop window.

And sometimes, after a bout of introspection, Lavender would thrust away her thoughts as mere emotional superficialities, and tell herself how possible it is for a woman to have soaring ideals, and insufficient brains to keep them company. And she would ponder miserably, and wonder if the crux of the matter lay in the fact that she had not the pluck to realise that she was but an ordinary person, without enough to do. Nothing more intricate than that.

When she found Maurois saying of Disraeli that it seemed to him that life would be intolerable were he not the greatest of men, she said : " That's me ! Well, he *did* become great. But what about me ? What can I do ? "

She saw that Dizzy's supreme vanity was assuaged by power ; and that his power was service to a country not even his. But it was service on a grand scale. That was what appealed to her : the Grand Scale. Not the publicity—that was incidental.

She might serve, but not on a grand scale. Service was the ultimate way Dizzy came to express himself.

Like Byron. They both tried to do it on paper. But they only reached the first stage of Romanticism which is Introspection, and not the final stage which is to be outside oneself. Lavender was sure of it. But this self-expression, she couldn't help its cravings. Once she had spoken to Johnny about it. He was sympathetic. Cravings? Yes, he knew them. Sometimes he felt a yearning for a bit of red mousetrap cheese, and could settle to nothing till he'd been to the larder and had it. But in Lavender's case there stood in the way of her cravings a lack of grasp and push. A restless laziness possessed her. She knew she couldn't write; her painting, though more successful than her father's, had no character, and her 'cello was going from bad to worse.

In playing, her imagination outstripped her patience. Her interpretation was extraordinarily good; but she had never entirely mastered certain elementary details of technique. The good man who taught her, coming from London to tour the desolation of the Provinces, said: " This slovenly brilliance will never give you any satisfaction. You won't tackle your initial faults for me. Perhaps you will do so in Paris. Perhaps you won't."

And what with the gloom inspired by him; the leapings of her imagination; her lack of success, both with Mammon and the Intellectuals; those sudden glimpses of poetry that disappeared so utterly; the conviction of her infinitesimal importance in the Universe; and the shavings of philosophy that tangled what faith she had—she felt that which Thomas Hardy once called " The Plight of Being Alive."

And one day, the last of Fenn's stay, they went over to play hockey at a house some fifteen miles away.

Their host met them, hoping they had brought a change of raiment and would stay to tea. And there, staying in the house was Mr. Compton-Mallett ; he that had given William such a lot of tepid trouble, and had been psycho-analysed as " fit for clerical work."

He was tall,with shifting black eyes that were too insolent to be called sly. They found him on the field before the game. Johnny and Fenn regarded him with interest. Lavender knew him, having met him at this house in the autumn ; Nigel addressed him. " And how do you do ? " he said playfully, with the self-confidence of a cordial dislike.

" Very well, thank you," snarled his erstwhile chum.

" My good boy," retorted Nigel in William's tones, " ' how do you do ' is a rhetorical question. We don't expect an answer." And he went on to ask how Compton-Mallett was enjoying Oxford with all its towers and spires.

He took the line of an ancient son of that City, steeped in memories. The undergraduate glowered. Was he in College ? No. How scurvy of the Authorities his first term to put him into digs. when he should be making a nice circle of friends for himself in College !

And where were his digs. ?   In Wellington Square ?
Ah, a pretty spot !   Granted it had not the grave
beauty of Tom Quad or Magdalen Tower, but there
was a something about it, an indefinable charm,
a *je ne sais quoi* ; and he invited Compton-Mallett
to agree with him.   And if he remembered rightly
it was there one opened one's window and listened
to everyone else's gramophones.   Yes, he once
knew an æsthete who lived there.   Slug whiskers
and a bottle-green overcoat.   No gramophone for
him !   He had an Æolian harp slung in his window.
And how had Compton-Mallett enjoyed Guy Fawkes
night ?

" Now who was it that told me you hit the
policeman and carried off four helmets and burst
a paper bag behind the Proctor's back ? "

Ah, well, boys would be boys, or rather he supposed he should say, men would be men ; and Nigel
waggled a finger at him.

" We are not amused, and don't show off,"
growled Compton-Mallett.

But Nigel said that he was amused, and asked
after Compton-Mallett's politics, and whether he
had any at the moment.   This caused laughter,
for it was widely known that Compton-Mallett was
passing through political distemper.   Lately, so
the news had been put about, he had left the Liberals,
and seeing red, disgraced his family by sitting hatted
throughout the National Anthem at the Opening of
a Parish Fête.   And during Nigel's catechism John
Fenn noticed Lavender exchanging glances of
sympathy and commiseration with Compton-Mallett.

Now, thought Fenn, she shouldn't do that. She ought to stick to Nigel, even though he is showing off. Fenn was quite put out. He tried to get things straight in his mind.

He remembered a remark of his mother's. Some people, she said, are constitutionally disloyal. Their disloyalty is not the vindictive brand, but is the outcome of weakness, sympathy, and a faculty for seeing the other side to the question. Now this is what we have here, thought Fenn. That evening he wrote to his mother. Of Lavender he said : " The poor child is a chameleon, and changes her whole character with everyone she meets. I've already seen about fifteen versions of her. She doesn't seem too happy in any of her rôles ; and I think her scraps of knowledge bother her. You must see her when she comes to Paris."

And returning from the hockey match Lavender regretted her sympathy with Compton-Mallett.

She wasn't such a fool, she told herself, as not to realise that he was one ; but she resented the publicity Nigel had given the poor creature's abortive politics.

And she continued very sorrowful until late that evening, when she roused herself, and by mistake told Johnny an amusing story that he had some time ago told her, and came upon the point prematurely to boot.

And Johnny laughed from the bottom of his heart. And she was bitter, and they began to quarrel sharply, and Mark told them to be quiet. One was as bad as the other, he said.

And at that nursery phrase Lavender came out of her shadowy unhappiness, telling Johnny to give over.

And he told her to have done, admitting handsomely that he was himself a poor raconteur. It was not long since he used to ask riddles, saying " When's a door not ajar ? "

And Lavender grew happier and happier, and began to talk about the school O.T.C. John Fenn drew her out, listened and explained, and saw the facets of her character, for he loved her, and went on to talk of Certificate A. Mark listened gravely. Nigel drowsed through the familiar technicalities. Johnny too had heard it all from Gray.

Whilst above, Lavender's Guardian Angel was chatting to John Fenn's, and said it gave him real pleasure to see the blind leading the blind so successfully for once.

But at this Fenn's Good Angel bridled, saying that Fenn was only purblind, and that he was pleased with him for seeing through Lavender so clearly.

John Fenn went away next day, taking Timmy with him.

Lavender respected him, for he had not taken to her at first sight.

*　　　*　　　*　　　*

At the end of March Lavender had a conversation with William, and the ground become more solid under her feet.

By the time she was twenty-five, she had forgotten whatever it was the poets upset themselves for ; and had forgotten how infinitesimal she was in the Universe ; for she became important to those about her, who counted on her for support and sympathy ; her father for one ; and Compton-Mallett to whom she became engaged for a short time, when he, with civic tumult, was returned Conservative Member for a town in the North.

Then came a year's quiet. After that, her marriage. And all the people, remembering how unaccountable she had been, and the way she used to turn the phrase about the things she did not understand—they said that it was a very good thing she had settled down at last.

PART II
HILARY

CHAPTER XIII

" Les agneaux sautillaient gauchement . . . le printemps était . . . revenu."—Tolstoy.

"THE Spring!" said Johnny, "it makes me stomach jump!" An exact expression of his feelings, not as yet snapped up by the poets.

It was after tea in February and he hung out of Nigel's study window, unable to settle down to anything, for he had it in his bones.

For there was a lightness in the sky and the birds were shouting; and there was that nakedness about the country-side that is unpronounced in winter.

Winter's bleakness is clothed in dimness about the trees; shut in by a low, iron-grey sky, or overcast by storms, or snug in fog, or under snow, or jewelled by frost.

But Spring is naked with nothing between it and heaven, and there was that evening a clear and restless cold, and snowdrops and what-not were pricking through the grass. Even William was pleased, and stepped out into the garden to sniff it all, and told Julia that he thought things were really very well arranged.

All four seasons, he said, were so distanced that every year they took him completely by surprise.

Each taste and smell as it returned was stranger than ever in its familiarity.

And he supposed that this was one of the things (like his back-chat with Fate) which kept him alive and spurred him on, to-morrow and to-morrow and to-morrow.

But Johnny continued to hang out of the window and listen to the birds ; and now and then he put in a whistle himself.

By and by Gray came in and told him he could clear away his tea-things. Johnny went off to do so.

Gray sat down comfortably.

Nigel was writing at the table.

After a while he looked up and stretched.

" About how many commas would you put to a page ? " he asked.

" What is it you're writing ? "

" An Editorial."

" Ah, then you'll need a good few. It's *style périodique* I suppose ? "

" Of course. One great fat cumulative sentence."

" Well," said Gray, " I'll look you out a nice quotation to lead off with ; and then you can work round via politics, economics, religion and moral science to the Public School Spirit, and fetch up with an indirect compliment to the Proprietor himself."

" Thank you, thank you," answered Nigel, " William has already given me advice."

William had.

When it came to his ears that Nigel was now
Editor of the Magazine, he said :

" Just mind you give us our usual turgid bombast,
my good boy. And then there'll be all those Minutes
of the Societies, with one or two ' we's ' to break the
monotony of the third person."

But Nigel said there would be innovations, and
gave William to understand that in this number he
would find a Comic Strip together with an account
of Rat Day; the ménus of last term's House
Suppers, and the caning averages of School Prefects
throughout the year.

He now repeated this to Gray, who offered himself
to write an article on Housemasters' Children :
Their Habits and Mode of Life.

He was no scribe, he said, but he'd heard that if
the matter came straight from the heart, the style
and turning of the phrase would follow as the night
the day. They talked a little of Housemasters'
children, and of Andrew in particular. Then Fenn
came in : Could one of them take the second half of
Preparation to-night, as he was going out ?

They stood up, their faces stiff with woe. Fenn
said he was very sorry about it, but that Penhurst
had suggested them.

Nigel motioned him to a chair and they all sat
down.

" Yes," said Gray, " Penhurst takes the whole of
Preparation himself once a week, in order to spot
malefactors. And the others have their special days
too. But when you go out, sir, it always comes down
to us dregs."

" You see," Nigel explained, " it's all right for you regulars ; they take you for granted ; but with us they try their tricks."

" Oh, but I've had trouble too," said Fenn.

" We don't mind attempted insubordination so much as when they want to know things," said Gray.

" Ah, yes," said Nigel sighing, " give me a nice, sleek prig, who knows what he's got to do, and rules a margin, and does it, and then wipes his pen and folds his clean hands in repose till the bell shall ring. Well, we'll toss for it to-night."

Fenn thanked them and stayed chatting.

Gray and Nigel sat on, doing nothing, very happily.

" Oughtn't you to be doing something ? " John Fenn was anxious, but disinclined to move.

" Oh no." And they explained how there was a satisfaction in wasting time deliberately. It was only when you were forced to do so, or kept waiting, that idleness was irritating and did you harm.

Fenn said : " Is that so ? " And twitched his eyebrows. By and by he went away.

" If he really thinks we ought to work, why did he stay hobnobbing ? He hasn't much to say. He's a silent man. William has drowned him in words."

" Well, personally I think we're all too cut-down here ; it's only William who talks," said Gray, who remembered how, years back, he had been seized, as some are, by the love of profuse apology for its own sake ; and once had stepped up to William and opened his mouth to begin ; when William said, flipping his fingers :

"My good boy, I don't want your confounded politeness," and had walked off, leaving Gray gaping.

Nigel got up and went to the window.

"Our Editorial will have to wait," he said. "I've got cramp to-night. Scrivener's palsy ; student's stoop and mental dyspepsia. I'd like to get out of here and walk till I drop, and then eat and drink and drink at a 'Public,' and go on walking to-morrow, and get down to the coast, and send William a picture postcard, and cross, and go on walking into France."

"You might take me along with you."

But Nigel said no. Gray would chatter and take little military steps ; and as it was Spring he would probably sing as well, which was like bath-water running away, and would upset the French lambs in the fields.

Nigel went on building castles in Spain. And as he stood there by the window, looking into the cold light, with the room growing darker behind him, he felt something, and it touched him fleetingly and was gone.

And because of it he drew in his breath. For in that moment he sensed the urgent sorrow of the Spring, and the pangs of it ; the pangs and wonder of a Resurrection ; an ancient pagan wonder, and a Christian one.

And then it was gone—a brief apocalypse, and his mind's eye closed again.

He turned round, for Johnny had come back, looking quite chapfallen.

"How now? What's the matter?" Gray asked. "Have you broken my Crown-Derby slop bowl?"

Johnny said no; he was just going off to be beaten.

"Who by? and what for?" said Nigel.

"Teacher. Because he can't find my essay."

"Did you ever write it?"

"No."

"Well," said Gray kindly, "you needn't droop. He won't hurt you. He's got no technique."

"No. None at all," put in Nigel, "one of the last of the old school of vicarious chastisers. Motto: 'It hurts me more than it does you.' And I should think it does—the way he sets about it!"

So Johnny went away enheartened, and found that it was as they had said; and came back from Throssell's House in a glow, and dashed off an essay for Warner in the heat of the moment.

And that evening his thoughts were in full spate. Away he went, untrammelled. For what is History but World-gossip?

So he treated Warner to a wealth of irrelevancies, astounding and disconcerting. And his most flagrant opinions he just popped into inverted commas, and left Warner to puzzle them out. His unruled margins he bespattered with dates.

He got it all done in twenty minutes and lay back panting.

Now let the man correct the stuff!

And here was enough side-tracking matter to last until the term's end.

He foresaw an orgy of questionings, explanation and debate, enlivened and sustained by his companions.

After that he took a rest, ranging over the future drowsily ; and he put the final touches to his day-dreams.

For he, too, had day-dreams ; lovely, material and copper-bottomed ones.

He anticipated the time when he should make money to burn, and could follow the strawberry season round ; for beginning in May in the South of France, he would make a progress northward, and finish up in Scotland late in August.

And he would be a King of Commerce and wave a cigar from the bottom of a leather arm-chair ; and his cigars should be as fat as plantains !

And he would write a prodigious Autobiography : My Life, by John Bentley. With a Preface by Johnny Bentley. And (like the work of the man in *Punch* who had so taken his fancy) the dedication would be : " To Myself ; without whose untiring energy and perseverance, this book would never have been written." And then copies would be given away signed: "From the Author to my Friend."

And he would build a Rest-house for Tramps, and it should be just one vast Bar-parlour. And he should go in rags himself in springtime, and saunter through the lanes, unshaven ; and thrust his great boot into other people's doors, swearing most sulphurously !

In his exuberance he chuckled and caught Gray's eye ; for Gray had lost the toss and was taking Preparation.

So Johnny quenched his smiles, and without ostentation drew a paper bag from his pocket.

Inside was a Treasure.

It was wrapped in linen with *Private and Confidential* scrawled in marking ink upon it.

Under the linen was a strip of paper, rolled from each end upon little sticks, like a Hebrew Scroll of the Scriptures.

But this was not a scroll of the Scriptures. It was a General Knowledge Paper, compiled by himself in recent years. But the questions were not framed for public enlightenment. They were for his own edification ; Private and Confidential, as it said.

And the scroll was to him as diaries are to other people, and secret poetry.

Information on the scroll was headed by a collection of Mediæval Oaths and synonyms for Hell and Drunkenness. Johnny read these through lovingly.

Then below he asked :

" Who said :

" The nose is the rudder to the face ?
" The child is father to the man ?
" We are seven ?
" Now we are six ? "

And then :

" Whose :

> " face launched a thousand ships ?
> " hair hung like flax on a distaff ?
> " smile was like a silver plate on a coffin ? "

Now came a higgledy-piggledy request to distinguish between :

> " Old Benchers
> " Old Stagers
> " The Vicars of Bray and Wakefield
> " Plymouth Brethren
> " Plymouth Rocks
> " Alf's Button
> " Lear's Button
> " The Boston Tea Party
> " The Mad Hatter's Tea Party
> " The Third Sex
> " The Fourth Dimension
> " The White Star Line
> " The Date Line
> " The Plimsoll Line
> " The Wooden Horse
> " The White Horse
> " The High Horse
> " The Blue
>> Red
>> Isosceles
>> and Eternal Triangles
> " A Bluecoat
> " A Blue-stocking
> " A black-leg

" A Pale-face
" A black eye
" A straight eye
" A bull's eye
" A glad eye
" Pink-eye."

And lastly between :

" Abraham Cowley
" Morris-Cowley
" Harvey Nichols
" Beverley Nichols
" Ambergris
&
" Verdigris."

And Johnny cherished the scroll and it grew in length as the years went by.

But now he put it away in his pocket, and dreaming, gleefully conceived another castle in the air ; his home above a valley.

And he would have two children, and call them Aloysius and Anastasia.

Chips of the Old Block they would be ; and in the Evening of Life, the Chips would warm the cockles of the Old Block's heart.

CHAPTER XIV

"We have done you bold and saucy wrong!"
—"*Othello.*"

WHEN Teacher's birthday came his wife gave him "The Mediæval Mind"—a great fat book—and in it he found: "What judgment hangs over those who act like buffoons with laughter and vain giggling . . . who give way to foolish mirth and vain jocularity; those who not only laugh themselves, but with scurrilities drag laughter from their listeners!" Teacher, glad that judgment hung over such people, hurried into school and suffered sharply from them.

The day was to blame; the sunlight and the pace of the clouds. And all above the din, Teacher said he thought he could still hear one or two people talking; and Bentley minor came up about his half-term Test Paper to regret that he was not responsible for what he wrote in an examination—it was like swearing under gas. Teacher loathed his confidential impudence and quivered like a blanc-mange.

The same set of scoundrels came again to Teacher two days later.

As ever, the more part knew not wherefore they

were come together ; and the rest in their impartiality brought no books, believing as they did in the unity of knowledge.

And learning was at a low ebb.

Teacher bore with them, and raising his voice, began introducing them to Wordsworth.

He told them about his boyhood and his school up in the hills, a wild free place it would seem ; and one or two of his pupils within earshot listened abstractedly as they scribbled noses and profiles, or embellished the carvings upon their desks.

And Teacher spoke of the man Wordsworth's general work, and said what a freshening thing it was that Literature should have come out of doors again, after that smug Cockney School.

And forgetting who they were and where he was, Throssell went on to say that Wordsworth was undoubtedly in blinkers, but that his one glimpse was both heavenly and true.

Here they lost the thread, but that did not disturb them ; and they turned round to have a look at one Clitheroe who had buttoned on his coat hind-part before, with the seat-back of his desk inside it ; and was fixed there—strange and bloated and shapeless, with inflated cheeks and a rolling eye ; a creature fit only for the summit of a bonfire.

And Teacher continued, looking neither to left nor to right, nor yet in front of him, but down at his books ; seeing beyond the print, perhaps, a wide stretch of Lake Country in its vividness ; its heights and gracious distances, and rain-washed airs. And maybe the steady murmur of the disturbance about him came to his ears as the reverberations of some torrent in the hills about Hawk's Head.

Be that as it may, the murmur was pierced by a question, shrilling up above the din :

"Was he that man that wrote ' The Idiot Boy,' sir ? "

Teacher came to earth, and truthful from childhood upward, resisted the temptation to tell Bentley that " The Idiot Boy," " We are Seven," and certain other pieces were written by another man of the same name.

But Johnny was interested.

Since he had come across him he remembered the Idiot Boy from time to time, and sympathised.

For who would not sympathise with an enterprising loon who gave his burbling mother the slip, and rode away off into the stark moonlight, for the whole of one long, blue night ?

Not that he should care to do that himself. The jaunt did not appeal to him.

He remembered his own terror that night in the autumn, swimming towards the North Pole. But that sort of loon, he felt, would be in tune with the moonlight, and all of a piece with something he could not name ; that panic loneliness.

So he excused the boy everything, even his burring lips, on account of his mother.

Besides, his name was Johnny, and that was in itself a bond.

The lesson progressed, and the monotony of its turbulence was only towards the end disturbed by Clitheroe's struggles to undo his coat.

M

But during the following week Teacher became aware of a change in the atmosphere.

There was a growing tendency to listen to what he had to say; and this troubled him; for the attention paid him by these Philistines was, he considered, out of all proportion to the significance, not of what he had to say, but of what his remarks could mean to their unopened minds.

The attention waxed subtle and mocking. Teacher viewed it with growing concern. It was quite different from anything he had hitherto undergone.

He told himself that it was all imagination, and chid himself for suffering from groundless fears. But as the days went by it was unfolded to him by looks, phrases overheard, the constant popping of corks, and by a series of oblique jests that he was regarded as a sort of Bacchus. Or was he the reincarnation of Pussyfoot Johnson? It seems incredible that he should not have known which, and still more singular that as a quiet and moderate drinker he should have been identified with either gentleman. And yet it was so.

He never knew how it came about, nor who was responsible for the elaborate network of legend and innuendo that now ensnared him. All he knew was, that alcohol was in the air, and life intolerable.

In his unquiet mind he went through his recent discourses and conversations, and found nothing that could have engendered so hideous an embranglement.

Within him festered his dismay and bitterness;

for he had an innate reticence and kept his few troubles to himself. To talk about oneself was as bad as dropping H's.

Besides, this affair was at once too trivial and too painful to be divulged.

So he kept silence, and during the ensuing week appeared punctually at his form-room door.

And the ruffians gushed in through a common entrance at the far end ; and Teacher came to know that this was now styled the " Jug and Bottle " ; nor was the knowledge intended to be hid from him. Whilst the fact of his bi-weekly hour with this set, beginning at nine, rather naturally gave rise to jesting at the close of it, when there were cries : " Time, please, gentlemen ! Ten o'clock. Out you go quiet ! " and such-like, echoing unpleasantly as he went down the corridor.

Nothing was safe from them. Nothing sacred. They even attacked Herrick, daintiest of poets, one of his acknowledged favourites, pronouncing his name with an inebriated hiccup.

And a portrait of Herrick was palmed off on him by means of much furtive yet ostentatious handing round.

Whilst realising his mistake in confiscating this, Teacher had ample time to contemplate the Poet's face, which was bibulous.

And returning late one evening for a book, he found scrawled upon the blackboard a crude parody of " To Daisies, not to Shut so soon," a reflection upon the Closing Hours, it would appear.

Until then these fiends had kept nominally inside

the law ; for none of their remarks could he prove to have been directly addressed to him.

But here was something down in black and white. Teacher resolved to speak boldly and trenchantly on the morrow, and lifted down the blackboard, placing it with care in a corner, the writing to the wall.

On the morrow he arrived early, only to find that the blackboard had been scoured by some officious manservant. Moreover, he was further put out by the appearance of the scoundrels, decorated one and all with blue ribbon bows.

His heart sank. Again he kept silence, thinking that although the Varsity Boat Race was yet a long way off, it would be enough to shelter them and their blue ribbon in the event of an inquiry.

But that afternoon, as he was walking sadly home from the golf links with the wind in his ears, he was overtaken by John Fenn, and they got talking, and Fenn said how lucky he thought him to be, teaching something plastic, like Literature, instead of a rigid thing like Elementary Chemistry.

Then Throssell, despite his reticence, said bitterly that at the moment he found no pleasure in teaching anything at all ; and out came his tangled tale of woe, of temperance, and alcohol, of " Jug and Bottle " and Blue Ribbon.

John Fenn heard him without interruption, and then probed him.

How long had this been going on ? Was any particular boy at the bottom of it, did he think ? Or boys from any particular House ?

Throssell gave him no help. His unwonted burst of confidence was now over, and he had withdrawn again into himself. All Fenn was able to gather was that the affair had come into being by spontaneous generation, a plague from Heaven which had settled on him, and would stay, as far as he could see, until Heaven saw fit to remove it. Fenn tried to rally him, suggesting a proper inquiry so that form masters might deal with these people ; or how about the Prefects ? But Teacher shook his head. He would not have his wounds any further disclosed.

He would go on as before. It was his own fault for not nipping the affair in the bud. But now it was in full flower, and he had not a leg to stand upon.

He continued, with grief, to mix his metaphors. He had, he said, been living in the clouds for years, unmoved by Middle School disorder ; content to wait till these young grubs should shed their ignorance and enter into the Sixth Form upon the wings of their new-found understanding.

But now, caught unawares, he had been stung.

And he besought Fenn to say nothing of this to any living soul.

But Fenn would not hear of leaving him in this trouble. The matter could be cleared up without delay.

" You leave it to me, sir. Your name shan't come in at all. It's not as far-reaching as you think. It hasn't spread to the other forms you take in the Middle School. And this lot probably never think of it except when they are with you."

In the end he left Throssell apathetic, but with a lighter heart.

Fenn thought deeply. Knowing Johnny to be in this English Set, and knowing Johnny, he thought more deeply.

That evening, a Saturday, he set about finding Nigel and Gray if possible. This was not easy, as the school were scattered everywhere. They were not in William's House, nor were they in the Library where Teacher addressed the Literary Society on Greek Art, opening with a lantern-slide of Apollo Belvedere upside-down.

Nor were they in Big School where trebles practised madrigals.

Fenn dropped into the Chapel. Bodies moved about in semi-darkness, and a Prefect was practising his Lesson for to-morrow. He kept saying : " *And He said unto them* . . ." in different pitch and strength of voice.

Nigel and Gray were not there.

But in the gymnasium he found them. The gymnasium was packed. At the farther end boxing was in progress ; whilst close by the door, up and down upon a strip of matting, Sergeant Kettle, his features obscured behind a sort of meat-safe, was giving fencing instruction in " loose play." His opponent, squat and bandy-legged, fought with a passionate lack of skill. There was a crash and rattle of steel. Fenn watched upon the fringe of the crowd.

" Who is that ? " he asked a boy beside him.

" It's Gray, sir," said the boy, who was laughing ;
" he's only just begun sabre."

And even as he said it, Gray and the sergeant
emerged from their meat-safes and shook hands.

" Ah, Mr. Gray," said Kettle, " you've a long way
to go yet." And he added that he'd never seen
such strokes outside a butcher's shop.

Gray mopped his face, panting. He had taken
up fencing late in life. A flimsy sport ! But he stuck
to it. Nor did he take Kettle's reproof in silence.

" Well," he said loudly, " I may not show up here,
but on Christmas Eve, when I was out buying a
gift for my old nurse, I was set upon by a sturdy
beggar twice my size, and I sent his false teeth
rattling down his throat with one lunge of my
parasol."

" That's as may be, Mr. Gray," said Kettle
hurriedly, making a note never in future to give
the boy a chance to bandy words. Him and 'is
dam' back-chat ! And going into the Army too !
Well, they'd learn him ! " But what you comes
here to learn is finesse," he said, thus clinching the
argument and pronouncing the aim of his teaching
to rhyme with a popular brand of Stout.

He then waved forward his next victim.

Fenn caught hold of Gray. " I want to speak to
you and Nigel some time this evening."

" Right, sir. We're just going down to the House.
Nigel's got a black eye. He'll need steak for it."

They pushed their way up the gymnasium towards the ring, where they found Nigel, with one
bright eye and a bleeding mouth.

"Yes, we're just going, sir," he said, and they collected their greatcoats and came out, the three of them, into the Parade Ground. Through the gymnasium windows the lights cast yellow squares upon the gravel.

There was rain in the air, and a wan moon shifting through the clouds.

On the way down to the House, Fenn told them of Mr. Throssell's predicament.

They listened.

At the end they began skipping about the road, from side to side in Pigling-Bland fashion, finger in cheek, popping corks.

Then they halted to lean against one another and laugh.

Fenn grew uneasy. It was no laughing matter, he said.

No, indeed, they agreed readily enough ; and Nigel said it was a scurrilous business, but that no one would benefit by a public inquiry.

"That's what I think," said Fenn, "and that's why I came to you. I'm certain Johnny's at the bottom of it."

"Ah, Johnny !" said Nigel darkly, adding that he would be warming his jacket for him.

"No," said Gray, "I wouldn't make an example of anyone. It gives too much importance to the whole affair. Besides, the warming of their jackets is too long overdue. No, I wouldn't do it that way. Make no inquiries. Ask no questions. It's of no consequence how it originated. *But* they must be paid in kind."

And he grew very excited, saying this was poor Mr. Throssell's private vendetta, which he personally would carry out, and serve those Blue-Ribbon Stalwarts as they had served poor Mr. Throssell. He only wished it were possible to drown the lot of them in Malmsey wine !

Nigel restrained him. " You can't just go and take charge like that," he said. " 'Tisn't even a House affair. Even then it would go to Penhurst, and we shouldn't be called in at all. Are we pleni-potentiaries ? "

But John Fenn urged that as it was so private and unusual a matter it should not be judged on precedent. Why not go to the Senior Prefect and to Penhurst, and arrange to take steps behind the scenes ? Apply for a mandate. And on second thoughts Nigel had better keep out of it, otherwise the Band of Hope might think Johnny had been gossiping.

This was finally agreed upon, and Gray quickened his steps, rubbing his hands ; for already, he said, he had a plan.

CHAPTER XV

" . . . He is clean contrary to our doings."—
The Wisdom of Solomon.

GRAY took steps.

On the following Monday he went down
to the village with Nigel, in that free hour between
dinner and games.

Walking briskly, they passed the ' King's Arms '
and turned down a cobbled passage, at the far end
of which stood its only rival, the ' Hind and
Panther.' It was an unsuccessful rival, and the
reasons for this were not far to seek.

Down its blind alley it was inaccessible and
dark. But this natural darkness was not the only
gloom that hung about the neighbourhood.

No. For the ' Hind and Panther ' was kept by
a man who had a brother who had gone and set
himself up as a Monumental Mason just over the
way. In fact, the Bar Parlour windows of the
fraternal tavern gave on the monumental building
yard, with its chilling vista of tombstones in
embryo. So no wonder the ' Hind and Panther '
lacked regular visitors. For who, when turning in
to drink and be merry, would not resent being thus
put in mind of his death on the morrow ?

Moreover, the finished stones were cocked up in great prominence all along the front of the yard.— " To the Glory of God, and in memory of . . ." and then would come a most distasteful blank. And as few among the villagers would leave the wherewithal for a special stone made to order, it was felt generally, life being so uncertain, that your last memorial was there waiting for you somewhere, grinning stark and white. And that, even if the Bar Parlour curtains *were* drawn, was enough to take the taste out of the beer.

So business was slack and mine host in consequence a sour fellow, and the brothers estranged, especially at this time of year, the bleak winter's close ; what with bells tolling, graves in the digging, and monumental orders pouring in. Now it was because of all this that Gray came to the ' Hind and Panther.'

For, as far as he knew, Kedge and the other school servants and gardeners went to the ' King's Arms ' ; and his visit here would be unlikely to come to William's ears.

So he came neither to drink nor to deceive William, but to hire beer bottles and avenge Teacher. Stepping up to the door, he rapped. After a while there were stirrings, and the Publican appeared in carpet shoes.

" Have you," asked Gray, " any returned empties ? "

' Hind and Panther ' blinked, and, blinking, expectorated out on to the cobblestones.

" ' Il crache loin ! ' " said Nigel to Gray.

" You come from the School, you do," said the man, and jerked a thumb in the direction of the place. " What'll you want with bottles ? "

" They're for an experiment." And they argued with him until he leased them a number of small brown beer bottles, and shambled off to fetch them. There was much about him of the animal disturbed in its hole.

Nigel looked up at the sky and smelt the March air, for to-day was the first of the month, and buds distinct upon the trees.

Gray said he would not have his evening pint here if he lived in the village. Give him the ' King's Arms '; and they turned round, leaning against the doorposts, and read the inscriptions on the tombstones over the way. They had just about made their choice when the Publican returned with bottles clinking in a sack, to drive his bargain.

" Back they come on Monday next, and you can pay the ordinary deposit : tuppence a bottle ; only I keeps the money, same as if you'd broke the lot. Any you do break'll be a penny on the tuppence."

Gray counted the money into his palm, where Nature's creases were emphasised by dirt. Nigel hoisted the sack over his shoulder ; and they set off homeward, carrying it in turn, and stopped to rest by a milestone at the bottom of the hill.

Nigel propped his feet against the lip of the ditch and leant against the bank, which was damp and set with primrose buds. Gray threw tufts of grass upon the road, and rehearsed his plans for avenging little Teacher.

They should be swift, dramatic, efficacious and cloaked in privacy.

Swift and dramatic they were—but his love of pageantry and showing-off betrayed him.

Through Johnny he gave orders for Teacher's Band of Hope to assemble in the gymnasium after dinner every day that week. There, carrying beer bottles, they marched and counter-marched and goose-stepped, until their heads swam ; and Gray dismissed them, saying : " To-morrow you'll please come at the same time and bring your blue ribbon bows. Collect those bottles." And he left them abruptly.

Immediately every tongue was loosed, and those in William's House set upon Johnny.

" You're his fag," they said ; " you've been talking ! "

Johnny swore passionately that he had never said a word.

" Well, what about your brother, then ? "

Again he swore, and at last convinced them. Until sleep stopped their tongues that night, the foul man Gray's name was on their lips. And would they go next day to the gymnasium ? Not they ; and some of them did not. Gray kept those present double time, and beat the absentees.

Next day as they goose-stepped, heads looked in at the windows to watch and laugh, nor did Gray send them away.

As always, an audience inflamed him ; and

abandoning privacy, he led his Blue Ribbon stalwarts out of the gymnasium and on to the Parade Ground.

There he was no longer the stern sergeant; and calling them all together, clapped his hands like some sprightly Playground Helper. They would, he said, play "Nuts in May," and play they did: Beer Bottles *v*. Blue Ribbons, and Gray made them sing, and would have no shirking, and kept crying out: "Enjoy yourselves!" so that boys passing joined the crowd. Backwards and forwards they tripped, and to have to sing was unendurable. When caught and questioned afterwards, they kept themselves to themselves, embittered, and would answer nothing.

Now a chatty, clear-voiced boy sat next door but three to Miss Greig at dinner that week, and told his neighbours all that he had seen, and all that they might see if they cared to come along with him to the Parade Ground.

Polly, duty calling, posted off to William to say she had not been able to help overhearing that boys were drinking beer in the Parade Ground after lunch each day, and that Gray was supplying it.

William said he was sorry to hear it, his eyebrows twitching north and south. "But why drink in such an exposed place as the Parade Ground?"

"You're not taking me seriously, Mr. Dean."

William said, Oh yes, he was, and rang the bell for Gray.

"You'll not find him—he is up at the Parade Ground," Polly faltered; but her composure returned when, after a long while, the manservant came back to say that Mr. Gray was not in the House. It was thought he had just gone up to Big School.

In William's ears a phrase sang before it came to her lips : " I told you so ! " she said, " and there you are ! "

" There I am *where* ? " William rose to wave his arms. " My dear lady," he said, " when you hear that *I* am not in the House and have gone into the village—do you, or do you not, give out that I am down drinking at the ' King's Arms ' ? "

" Of course not, Mr. Dean ; but that's no parallel to this case, where I have evidence."

" Evidence ! Evidence ! from a tuppenny-half-penny, niminy-piminy little boy, talking to his friends four or five places away from you at dinner ! "

" Straws show the way the wind blows, Mr. Dean."

" Very well, then," said William, really angry, " I will go up myself and see ; and perhaps you will wait about to attend to Gray when I bring him back on a hurdle ! "

He flung a muffler round his neck and stamped off up the road to the Parade Ground.

In he came at the gates, and lifted up his eyes. Heaven knows what Polly expected him to see ; and gazing at boys crowding over what should have been a quiet, deserted place, he swore his eyes deceived him. These were the creatures of her suspicious fancy ; a mirage ; a trick of the brain.

And the mirage bawled with laughter and pressed forward, watching something in the centre of the throng.

There, flushed in the face, the Band of Hope played " Wine and Water " (an alcoholic and tee-total version of " Oranges and Lemons "), and Gray directed, pacing arrogantly upon his toes ; while to one side, upon the sacred gravel of the Parade Ground, was a mound of empty beer bottles ; William stared at them—his heart turned to jelly.

Numb and unperceived he hurried home, and went straight up to his dressing-room. There, at least, he would be safe from Miss Greig.

After tea, as Penhurst was eating muffin over his fire, Nigel came in.

" We've mucked it," he lucidly explained. " William's sent for him, and he's been in there over half an hour already."

" Sent for who ? Gray ? "

" Yes, and now there'll be a grand inquiry, and Teacher's troubles exhumed."

" Then Gray's a bloody fool," Penhurst broke out. " He *will* show off. He can't put these things through quietly. You both of you do nothing but show off. And Fenn's another fool for meddling. I should have stamped out this damn silly business myself from the start. And now, with explana-tions, it'll last till the end of term. Wait and see what Gray says when he comes out, and then get hold of Fenn. And don't start helping any other masters out of their difficulties. If Fenn can't put things straight I'll see William myself."

What Gray said when he came out took twenty minutes.

William's shocked fury had come down on him like a storm of hail.

"I couldn't get one word in—he *would* confuse Reason with Excuse—they always do. I spoke up and 'Sir'-ed him hard, and he 'Sir'-ed me back— like Boswell and Johnson. I began badly. When I went in the sun was on him through that little leper's squint window, and his face was all screwed up—I thought he was smiling—that put me wrong from the start. *Do* you know, he thought we'd been drinking out of those bottles?"

Nigel said it all went to show you couldn't be too careful

Gray continued: "Then he turned icy-calm, and said he'd have the whole story again from the beginning. And I tried to make sense of it, keeping Teacher's name out. I didn't mention Fenn. He can settle with William as he pleases. Oh, but he was rude, William. 'The sooner I realised that prefectorial status could not be reconciled with that of public Clown, the better for me, and the better for the House. Clowning! Just living on a reputation for humour. And living on your reputation's as bad as living on your capital.' He does love turning the phrase."

And William had in common with all schoolmasters that Kant-like habit of maximising the action; and had rounded off his upbraidings with the inevitable: "What do you suppose would happen if everybody behaved like you?"

Then Gray remembered something which brought him near to whimpering:

N

"And you've not heard the worst," he said with drooping mouth. "I've got to take those—those —bottles back to 'Hind and Panther' before early school to-morrow. It's too bloody."

It was.

William lent him Kedge's wheelbarrow, and he set off rumbling down the hill.

Then the pin came out of the wheel, and he was derelict in the middle of the road.

And coasting down the hill in the keen morning air, came Sergeant Kettle, bound for the village on business connected with the school ; and his brakes being not all he thought they were, he, swerving by, caught the edge of the wheelbarrow, which overturned, knocking Gray prostrate. Gray sat amongst broken bottles. Kettle himself took a cruel toss ; and the ditch (William's Pig-ditch) received him and his cockled bicycle.

Kettle sat in the ditch for some time, talking below his breath.

Nor was that quite all.

For John Fenn saw William ; and William, hearing everything, wished to see Johnny, Clitheroe and certain others in his House. They came to him that evening, a Saturday, just a week since Teacher had made a confidant of Fenn.

They stood apprehensively outside his study door, undecided as to who should knock. Bentley had better, on the whole, they thought. And Johnny stood gazing at the door, grained and varnished, choosing a spot to knock upon.

As they waited, a grandfather clock struck seven,

and Andrew, William's eldest, came out of the passage leading to the kitchen, crossed the hall, and mounting the stairs, paused to eye them apprehensively.

He was in his dressing-gown, having refreshed himself in the kitchen.

Traces of his supper adhered to his face.

He had had a fine day ; it had begun with the brownest egg for breakfast, followed by a visit to the chicken-run to dangle bacon-rinds through the wire netting, while the hens ran about hysterically below. These were not Julia's prize Orpingtons. *They* were housed in style at the other end of the orchard. These were Kedge's domestic fowls, fattened like the pigs on House-scraps ; things pushed aside by Johnny and his friends. And these birds were sold at profit at each term's close. So were the pigs.

The rest of Andrew's Saturday morning, a holiday, had slipped pleasantly away ; and sweets had been bought down in the village in the afternoon.

There was cocoa for tea. A skin had formed. And a lump of brown sugar placed upon its wrinkled surface was allowed to sink slowly, enfolded in a skinny shroud.

After tea Andrew sharpened his penknives, and rolled about singing on the nursery floor.

And then, crushing soap down the waste-pipe, he took his bath.

Now, fed to the teeth, he was going upstairs. Over the banisters he looked down upon his Papa's boarders below.

" I know what you're goin' in there for ! " he said.

" I'm sure you don't," retorted Johnny crisply, below his breath.

" I don't know what you've done ; but I know what father'll do to you ! "

This he illustrated with gesture.

A quiver of rage passed over the group.

Johnny tiptoed over to the banisters.

" You've got a lot of food on your face."

(With hauteur Andrew turned his back.)

" And you're so fat we can see your cheeks from behind."

There were titters.

Of a sudden the study door opened.

" What's all this ? " William inquired sharply. " Andrew, what are you doing down here ? Go upstairs."

His firstborn sped away out of sight, and William turning to the party, waved them inside.

His study door closed upon them.

CHAPTER XVI

" L'ontogenèse reproduit la phylogenèse."
—AUGUSTE COMTE.

" On l'écoutait avec ravissement, car il disait des choses fort obscures."

DURING the week-end the weather changed to storms and a wind blowing bitterly over the early flowers.

And as Spring crept back again into hiding, William took occasion to point out to Warner that the moods of Nature were not to be trusted.

They were in Common Room, correcting books.

Warner said : " What's all this I hear about Throssell being ragged ? Something to do with bottles it was."

" Buz ! Buz ! " exclaimed William. " Throssell being ragged !   Throssell's been ragged these twenty years, and you've not heard of it ? "

" Of course I know he's ragged. But this was some special case. Something about your little Bentley and these Bottles, and Gray came into it somehow as well."

" Bottles ? Bottles ? " and William said he didn't know where Warner could have got that from. " But talking of that younger Bentley . . ."

But Warner persisted. " There must be something in it," he said, " because I met Kettle just now, and he was all bandaged up. It appears he had a bicycle accident on the hill on Saturday morning. Grazed his chin and forearms. He said he ran into Gray, who was pushing a wheelbarrow, and when it overturned, a lot of bottles tumbled out of a sack, and broke all over the road. Beer bottles, I think he said they were."

And William said it was a most extraordinary tale, and he would make inquiries.

He then went on to talk earnestly about the boy Bentley.

Warner listened indifferently. So Dean was not going to let him into this Throssell and bottle mystery.

Now Warner respected a man like Throssell who kept himself to himself; but here was one both garrulous and secretive. The worst type. And he looked William up and down, while William's flow of talk increased :

" His mathematics now. I don't know what's come over him and his work." It was of Johnny William spoke. " I purposely gave him no remove last term because he seemed in such a fog. Yet here he is in the same set, doing the same work and making the same mistakes, just automatically. He takes a bitter pride in getting on the wrong track to work away, page after page, smeary rough workings ; impassioned crossings-out ; and then finishes with something ludicrous—utterly ludicrous —and writes in triumph at the bottom : ' But this is impossible.' Like Burke, the brat delivers fifty truths in arriving at a false conclusion."

"And he's right," concluded William unexpectedly, with noddings of the head : "reason is not one of the richer faculties. I've always said so."

Silence at last. Warner got up to go.

"Oh, but his geometry ! " William burst out in a renewed effervescence of discourse. "In drawing diagrams I've never known that boy not choose a special case. And how does he work for you ? "

But Warner, never one of William's best listeners, was gone.

William finished by himself. That child would try and take down History at one gulp, like Holinshed and H. G. Wells. He chose his own thoughts and was sure of everything save mathematics, and knew which way he wished to go. He even planned out his ragging in form. Look at this affair of Throssell's ! He was a law to himself. And he had his private universe. For Johnny had once told William that he himself held to the Ante-Copernican system. It was, to his thinking, simpler and more in keeping with what he had first thought about the earth. It satisfied him ; and William agreed that as Johnny was not going to teach geography or astronomy, he was quite at liberty to hold the earth immobile.

And that day, as William thought of him, Johnny's spirits rose.

He had thrown off the effects of the Alcoholic

Embroglio ; and his Private and Confidential General Knowledge Paper was filling up. Recently, too, he had acquired a set of bright novel-jackets for his school books ; and this morning in Frog's lesson he had had a rare success at the back of the room, reading passages of Virgil aloud in broad Norfolk.

As for his mathematics, figures still appalled him. But if their secrets were not to be revealed to him —well, they were not. And he was not worrying. Certainly he did not relish being left down in the same set. He detested those who now learnt with him, and was surprised at their superior grasp of the matters in hand.

For, up to the present, he had considered that boys below him in the school were *ipso facto* of less intelligence than he.

But he disregarded these upstarts and scribbled out his preparations.

He had an old book, tattered and frayed, handed down from generation to generation.

On every page were scribblings, underlinings and remarks—his heritage. For there were answers written in, and hints and warnings ; for of what use is it to know an answer, if unable to arrive at it convincingly ?

And these remarks were written in the same spirit that prompts tramps to mark the gate-posts of the penurious, and hotel servants their luggage. A good turn done those in the same trade ; a fraternal kindliness found in those who have enemies in common.

After dinner Johnny went into the gymnasium to be weighed.

There was a full month before the end of term, but Kettle had to get forward with the business, and fill in his reports.

This afternoon Kettle was in no very pleasant temper.

His grazed forearms burned, as did his chin, which was latticed with sticking-plaster, and he was tired to death of explaining that he had not cut himself shaving.

He weighed all the A's.

Then he was held up, for Bentley came next on the list, and he was half-way up a rope, feet first, swinging about aloft ; supporting the Darwinian theory in his every movement.

Kettle roared to him to come down, and the plaster tightened across his angry facial muscles.

Johnny slithered to the ground and ran across to the scales.

Kettle said he thought he ought to know by now that no apparatus was to be used unless he himself were by.

" Ah, but you were by," said Johnny blandly, and he looked down at Kettle's face and asked him if he had cut himself shaving ?

Kettle growled, and then discovered with wrath that he had weighed Mr. Bentley with his shoes on. Johnny, apologising, took them off and stepped dreamily back on to the scales with one in each hand.

With infinite care Kettle obtained the same

result, and then caught sight of those shoes dangling by his nose as he knelt by his weighing-machine. He became very rude, saying here was Mr. Bentley's mentality in a nutshell !

At last Johnny went down at seven stone twelve ; and when the C's were done he slipped away with Clitheroe back to William's House to watch the photographing of the House XV—postponed from the end of last term on account of the fogs. Behind a laurel bush they went, and peeped out through the leaves.

Preparations were going forward ; people came out from the House with chairs, hanging about in the wind, chilly in their shorts. Gray, the Captain, was there pointing and directing, along with William, and a fiddly little man with a tripod, who kept disappearing beneath a black cloth.

There was a coming and going of boys who had forgotten to change into their football boots ; and William, cold and impatient, kept taking out his watch and glancing up at the sky.

And what a day for photography ! Uncertain light and hurrying clouds. William thought it too paltry to postpone the business all these months, and then to fall upon a day like this ! Still, the affair was in the boy Gray's hands, and if this year's XV came out like sons of Ham from Darkest Africa— as they would do, in this light—the boy had but himself to blame for his arrangements.

Yet what delay !

William fretted up and down whilst this good

Mr. Whatever-he-called-himself rearranged the seating and stepped back to view the effect with his head on one side, and then went to earth again beneath his pall.

At length William went up to the little creature and intimated that, as night was coming on, any further holding off would necessitate a flashlight group instead.

The footballers began to giggle, but the little man said that was reely alright now, if only the Young Gentlemen would keep still. He stood poised, with the bulb in his hand. And now here was Gray in the centre, refolding his arms!

The remnants of William's patience forsook him.

" My good boy," he exploded, " this is not a Wedding Group, nor are you the Bridegroom, and will you please keep still ! "

Later that same afternoon the junior heats for the sports were run. Johnny got a place in a hundred yards under fifteen. As he stood panting after it, John Fenn came up.

" If," he said, " you hadn't been a silly little clown, and had practised starting as I told you to, you might have won that heat."

Johnny got his greatcoat and accompanied Fenn to the Long Jumps, where Nigel and others were practising. Johnny enjoyed the sight.

And very entertaining it was—the frenzied way they ran and took off ; their frenzied faces ; their breathing ; their landings, and the way in which they came off the sand, and, returning to try again, glanced nonchalantly over their shoulders at the mess they'd made !

Nigel saw them and came over to them.

He had been up to Oxford for his examination, returning at noon in time for the photographing of the XV.

Fenn asked how he thought he had done.

Nigel said he thought he had not done well enough to get a scholarship. On the other hand, he had done well enough to obviate the arrival of a letter from Authority to the Headmaster asking why this boy was sent up for a scholarship—as had happened in Compton-Mallett's case.

" And I saw Compton-Mallett," Nigel went on ; " he was staying up for his Law-Prelim., I think. Haughty in his sub-fusc. ! So I hitched alongside and was at his elbow all the way up Hell Passage. And yesterday I stepped round to Wellington Square to look him up again. Such revelry there ! Eatin' and drinkin' and lights and loud voices and snatches of music ! And as I was hunting for his digs, a silver dish-cover comes hurtling out of an upper window—straight by my face in the darkness. And then the landlady to look for it, with a spotted dog at her heels. They came out of the upper window ? Oh, no. They came out of the door, and left it open, and I could see men pounding down the stairs inside. I laughed so much I had to cling on to the railings, and then a cat started singing in the boscage behind them. Oh, Wellington Square ! A rare spot. I pray God I may live there some day."

Johnny's eyes grew round with delight.

" You lived there, sir, didn't you ? " Nigel asked
Fenn.

" Yes, I did. But, look here, Nigel, what
happened in your interview ? "

" Oh, that. Well, there were a lot of holy men
sitting round a table. And me there with them,
making the best of myself when questioned. Very
civil I was."

" Yes, yes, yes. But what sort of questions did
they ask you ? " John Fenn was impatient.

" ' Do you drink ? ' for instance." Softly Johnny
put the suggestion.

" Nothing so pertinent." Nigel sobered down
and scratched his head. " Well, they were the
ordinary sort of questions. Just the kind I'd
always heard they asked. Just the sort you were
asked, I expect, sir. What you had done ? What
you were going to do ? And what you would be ?
They couldn't get much out of me. I wasn't
reticent. I was just barren. But they went on
questioning for a very long time ; so long, in fact,
that one of them, a little less holy than the rest,
and younger, launched a scrap of paper that went
from hand to hand. As far as I could see, he'd
drawn the face of the clock. I expect he wanted
his tea. I wanted mine. It was five o'clock."

John Fenn left them, and they walked down to
the House together, laughing over the photographing of the XV. And Nigel gave Johnny a
letter from Lavender he had found waiting for
him at Oxford, to wish him luck.

They turned into the gates of William's House, and separated.

At tea that evening Penhurst came in and gave out that the first half of Preparation would be in Studies, on account of a rehearsal in the dining hall.

For William was coming to give his opinion on the cubist scenery for the House play, and then to watch the rehearsal of a Curtain-raiser.

And here was William surveying the back-stage scenery, and saying it put him in mind of the Mappin terraces at the Zoo.

Then a curtain rolled down; other theatrical properties were put on the strip of stage before the footlights, and William's Curtain-raiser began.

William stood in the gloom at the far end of the dining-hall, his hand cupped behind his ear, to see if he could hear anything at all. Down there with him stood the chief electrician, and Miss Greig, who was very kindly going to consider clothes, and had made herself familiar with the lines of the Mongolian skull with a view to make-up. Gray would be simple, with his high cheek-bones. Bentley more difficult. And as she went on talking, William told himself this was the longest day he'd ever lived through. And it wasn't over yet. There was still Throssell's dinner-party to come.

Nigel reached his study door after the rehearsal.

" You can't come in now," he told Gray. " I've no time for your chat."

" You surely aren't going to work *now* ? " Gray was incredulous.

" Of course not. My education's closed until
October if I've got in. But William's lent me some
Byzantine Memoirs ; I want to finish them to-
night. They make me smile. Besides, I've got to
take the rest of Prep."

Gray became indignant.

" What ? Is this man Fenn going out again
to-night ? "

" They all are, except Polly. They're dining with
little Throssell. They'll be off quite soon. William
was already dressed at the rehearsal. I saw his
boiled shirt gleaming down there at the bottom of
the hall."

Nigel crossed to his window and drew back the
curtains. Yes, out in the courtyard Kedge was
getting the car to go, and very troublesome it was,
this cold night. He had barely jerked it into life
when his master appeared, waving a torch.

" Is that car ready, Kedge ? "

It was. And William called over his shoulder
to the others. They had better come along. It
was late enough as it was.

Julia came out with her music under her arm,
and John Fenn behind her.

The car moved off, turning slowly in the courtyard.

" Why," asked Nigel, " do William's headlights
squint like that ? And point to heaven ? I hope
they get there safe."

He let fall the curtain.

Outside, Kedge closed the doors of the Barn,
blowing upon his chill fingers.

Five minutes later, William and party were shown into Teacher's drawing-room ; a wide, low-ceilinged room with a Morris paper and long green curtains. And there were screens, a heavy *portière*, high-backed chairs, and bulbs in pots about the place ; and a grand piano open ready for Julia. Mrs. Throssell came forward to welcome them in her strong, deep voice, and drew Julia in to the fireside.

Teacher peeped out from behind her, his baldness shining.

"Well, William," he said, "the glass is falling. What is it doing outside ? "

And William said it was as cold as charity.

Presently they went in to dinner.

They sat—Julia on Teacher's right ; William on Mrs. Throssell's right ; and Clovis-Abel opposite John Fenn, facing him across the table, a pool of light.

Over the soup Teacher told William he was going for a few days' walking tour in the Bernese Oberland at Easter, before joining his wife at his brother's villa in the Euganean Hills.

"Switzerland ! " exclaimed William. "What do you want to go there for ? " A shut-in country it was, he said, and its people had shut-in minds. "Why don't you go to Tyrol if you want mountains ? "

Just as other people say "hounds," William said plain "Tyrol," aggressively ; and "Acts of Apostles," having excellent reasons (which he enjoyed giving) for the omission of the article.

But this time he was unchallenged.

It was not worth going into the matter.

Live and let live.

And they all had their whims of speech.

John Fenn's Greek was queer.

Clovis-Abcl mangled our language, and—exiled—forgot his own day by day.

Mrs. Throssell's grammar was sound, but she said " Dantë " and " Meccah " very strangely; and " Bagdad ": " Bug-dud "; while Teacher himself pronounced Rome to rhyme with " bomb " as in French.

" My good William," said Julia, " what do you know of Switzerland ? "

Indeed, William's experience was confined to a week's stay on the blue rim of Lake Leman, in an hotel styled " de l'Univers et de Portugal." But he stuck to his views, propounding them. And they all sat round with glassy eyes. Julia was considering sending William away alone at Easter to fish and forget he was a schoolmaster. Mrs. Throssell thought of the journey out to Italy; and Clovis-Abel of the term's end, and Paris in the spring.

And John Fenn was back where he had been this time a year ago, in the Jura; a field running up to a pine wood. On his back on the grass, with the snow scarce melted, and the sun hot upon the moss and primroses. Below lay little farms among bleak vineyards on the lower slopes; and across the Lake, Savoy and the white towns of France, and the sky hurrying over the mountains. On his left were larches, and through them from his height, he looked down to woods below, transparent, thin, with red-brown glooms and purple shadows.

And he had been reading " Anna Karénina." He had got to where someone advised putting rum on the paper coverings for jam-pots ; and it was there he had stopped reading to listen to the wind approaching through the pine wood—and, coming and coming, it never reached him !

A queer thing, noticed by Coleridge.

Then from this violent spring in the mountains, he came back an immense way to Throssell's table, to find William still telling Throssell where he should go for his holiday. But Teacher, smoothing his rare hairs, said that arrangements were already made.

And Teacher was not happy.

Unlike Johnny, he had failed to throw off the effects of that Alcoholic Imbroglio.

Now Fenn had sworn he should hear no more of it. No more he had, save indirectly ; yet peace and security had departed from his life.

He no longer took himself for granted. He watched his fellow-creatures, expecting derision, and he got it, together with indirect reminders of his sufferings. This morning, for instance, men came up from the village to attend to his telephone wires, and had accosted him in the luncheon hour, asking him for a jug of tea.

They only wished, they said (winking and grinning amongst themselves), that they could go down to the ' King's Arms.' But, you see, if they was to take a drop of something strong, and then go up a ladder and fall off it, they'd not get a penny Insurance, not if they was as sober as priests ; not if it 'ud been known they'd just had a drop of something strong !

And Teacher felt them to be mocking him. Yes. And the whole world was probably laughing at him, and here he was, at fifty-nine, discovering it ! He went on with his dinner, saying very little to Julia.

Then came Trifle in a silver bowl, and with it an intimation from the cook :

The sherry had been left out by mistake.

" How very nasty ! " said Teacher, and when it arrived he pecked at his pussyfoot Trifle—clammy and unpalatable stuff !

Alcohol : Blue ribbon—what twinges they both gave him still !

He looked up and caught John Fenn smiling at him ; a companionable smile, guessing his thoughts. And suddenly the cloud lifted for good and all, and was blown beyond his horizon. He saw the affair in its true light, and oh, the delightful unimportance of it all, and of them all, and of himself !

Broadly he smiled back at Fenn ; his habitual peace of mind returned to him at last.

Now again he could read and walk and talk in quiet enjoyment.

He could live through the noise they made in the Middle School ; and every hooligan would change in time, and listen.

His outlook brightened steadily. He beamed round his table. The sun was out again.

And lastly dessert.

In Mrs. Throssell's finger-bowls were flowers, tight-furled, of painted wood-fibre ; Japanese trifles, and they were slowly unfolding in the water.

Her husband touched them with his forefinger. One had not seen such things since one's nursery days, he said.

" Nursery days ! " William exclaimed. " I never had pretty things like this to play with when I was a child. They gave me few toys and no sweets. Plain and simple they brought me up. I was never spoilt. None of us were. Never encouraged to make naïve remarks about Angels and Paradise or anything of that sort. No."

He brooded, remembering.

" And the meals ! " he went on. " The way we used to gulp milk ! And when I left things on my plate they would say : ' There's many a poor child in the street who'd be thankful for that, Master William ! ' Oh, yes, and there were corners in my nursery, and dunces' hats, and how briskly we used to fight and tussle ! I fancy I exploded the fallacy that it takes two to make a quarrel ! My bitterest brawls were when the other party would not be provoked."

Round came the port, and the servant offered William a tangerine.

" Yes," William continued, " and how real Satan was then. When I was good, it was more to spite him than to please God. Satan was always hanging about then. In fact, I quite miss him now. And I used to defer the resistance of temptation until the very last minute ; to give him a sporting chance ! So you see," he said, turning to Mrs. Throssell, " just as my hand closed over the forbidden fruit or whatever it was, I would decide not to take it after all ; and that, I calculated, would make him gnash his fangs far more than if I had put the suggestion from me directly he'd made it. Poor fellow, kept waiting about, kicking his hoofs, and then me not obliging him in the end ! Ah yes, what times we had together, to be sure ! "

William sighed deeply and promised Mrs. Throssell to speak no more of the Devil that evening, at any rate before the servants.

Mrs. Throssell then told of her childhood, and Clovis-Abel of his, too. When he was small, his older relations died often, he said ; and then he was put into socks with black tops—*chaussettes deuil*. And he loved them.

" Um," said William. " Deaths of relations. A great feature of childhood. My grand-uncle now, he died in October and was buried on the day of the Cesarewitch.

" Now we lived in those parts, and down we came to Newmarket, my brothers and I from school, for the funeral, in the thick of the Cesarewitch crowd ; I'll never forget the day. And I hope the old man knows how we enjoyed it."

Teacher told William he must have been a grim and primitive child. He meant nothing in particular by the phrase and was only rounding off the conversation. But William took him up :

" Primitive ! Of course I was primitive, and you too, and all of us. What did Shelley say ? " And he told them what Shelley said, and they listened, for William rarely quoted, holding it the last stage of intellectual hypocrisy.

And Shelley said : " The savage is to ages what the child is to years."

Teacher pricked up his ears and began to rumble in class-room fashion : " That falls into line with Comte," he said. " He held that the development of the individual is reproduced in the development of the race. So . . ." he tapped the table with his finger.

But William broke in, very animated, gesticulating as though he were at the hustings.

" I know, I know," he exclaimed, " and Comte's right. Look how it fits. If a young child is a vandal, then the mediæval outlook is found later in the child of about ten, spoon-fed with religion ; whose celestial motives are entwined with bestial behaviour, and who is just beginning to throw off some of the fears and witchery and make-believe of childhood.

" The rest of the Dark Ages appears in that phlegmatic indifference we see so much of until the age of about fifteen or sixteen."

Here Teacher nodded vigorously ; but Julia said :

" My good William, the Dark Ages weren't phlegmatic."

" Beg pardon. Nor they were." William recanted glibly. " But they were busy and cruel and colourful and inconsistent and unselfconscious. Childlike in fact. But their close was unenlightened."

William continued : " Adolescence corresponds to the Renaissance ; and the Romantic Poets lived continually in the renaissance of their lives.

" At the present time," he went on, " the race has reached the stage of the young pup in his twenties . . ."

(Here everyone looked at John Fenn, and laughed.)

" . . . who is rapidly developing and feels he must be free, and is therefore agin' the government ; agin' religion, morality, authority, etc. etc. etc. And it's a pity, Fenn, that you don't bear out my remarks."

John Fenn grinned.

" Sir," he said. " I've heard you make all the Pessimist's remarks except ' What are things coming to ? Is it because of these theories that you didn't say that ? "

William thought gravely and said, Yes. He used to think that the attitude of the present age was accidental and brought about entirely by the War. But now he thought of the War as a contributing circumstance. And what were things coming to ? Well, it was obvious what things were coming to ; these times would pass. The race would slip into the level-headedness of its middle-age ; and finally into the wisdom and understanding of its old age, it was to be hoped.

And then, presumably, there would be a decline and fall into senility, trampled upon by some other rising race. And there you were.

William finished, regretting that he knew so little of the racial history of the Asiatics and the sons of Ham.

He would like to apply Comte to them and see if their histories tallied with their lives.

"How do you account for the Victorian Era, William?" asked Julia.

"Ah, that. But you can't apply that to Europe as a whole. Like Puritanism, it's a special case. It had no hold outside England and Germany."

Throssell said he thought perhaps it corresponded to that steady piety that appears now and then in the young, but not in the general run of them.

Mrs. Throssell, catching Julia's eye with difficulty, gave the sign to rise.

She did not approve of the events of hundreds of years being labelled off-hand in this manner.

Coffee they took, later, in the drawing-room, and William, who had nothing more to say for the moment, lay back in his chair, a little apart, behind an occasional table.

He was tired.

Julia went to the piano, and there was Clovis-Abel, as always, asking for Chopin.

Julia played a Mazurka. She could. She had the temperament.

William listened with mixed emotions. She had not played that thing for over a year. And then it had been in his study the day of the Grand Treacle

Explosion, when Mrs. Turvey had burst in, wailing incoherently of disaster in the kitchen.

For a great tin of syrup had been put to warm on the stove, with the lid on ; and this, at boiling-point, had burst, spraying the walls, scalding a kitchen maid, and sending the whole crew into flapping hysterics.

A nice day that had been. The music brought it back to him.

At the close of the Mazurka, Clovis-Abel rose to go.

He was to meet his " Stratteford-atte-Bowes " concerning some change in the Time-table.

" And tell them from me," said William, " that my last period on Thursdays is ruined by Phonetic Retchings next door. I don't know which of them is responsible."

Then William rose and said he must be going too. He must go back to the House.

" But why ? when there's Penhurst and Miss Greig in charge.

" I know. It's not that. Penhurst wants to see me. I told him I'd come back directly after dinner."

His hostess remonstrated further ; but William said she must not take on so. They were four for Bridge without him, as it was.

" But I was not going to play."

" Ah, but you will now, won't you ? And thank you for my good dinner."

" William, what about the car ? " asked Julia.

" I'll walk home."

" Yes, but it's so damp for your pumps."

" Oh, I'll tread as dainty as a cat."

He came into the room again in his greatcoat.

" Julia, you must be careful driving home. The brake is dicky ; and remember the barn doors are shut, whatever they may appear to be by the head-lights. Fenn, would you mind tucking a rug over the bonnet ; and one thing more : will you please place your seven-league boots nearer the wall out-side your door, so that I may not rouse the whole House stumbling over them on my way to bed."

" What a nasty, murky place your House sounds, William." And Teacher put on his spectacles to deal cards.

" Yes," said William, " naked gas-jets bending in the draught. Good night." And he closed the door.

Coming out into the night he found it to be snowing steadily ; slow feather-flakes. The wind had sunk.

He picked his way home and found Penhurst waiting in his study.

They sat down, and together they mapped out a boy's future.

The boy was to leave at the end of the term.

William and Penhurst had urged the Headmaster to get rid of him.

In William's mind the boy's life was now settled. All that remained to do was to thrust it upon him and keep his parents in check.

For William's mind leapt ahead.

To-morrow he and Penhurst would see the Headmaster. The boy was good with his hands. He must be got out to Bramble, an old boy in New South Wales.

Bramble, certainly a fussy Martha of a prefect in his time, had nevertheless a steady head on him. He wrote to William frequently, and to other people too, complaining that William would dump his scum and dregs upon him. In the last five years he had launched no less than six unsatisfactory boys.

Well, the boy in trouble should go to him, thought William, and be worked right off his legs.

Almost William looked up train and steamboat services !

And then this hastiness left him, and looking back he thought over Adolescence.

A heartrending time of discovery and stirrings ; a quickening and a striving to create.

A unique time, with Heaven and Hell suddenly disclosed.

A time when the best and the worst are commingled, as they are in those strange faculties, Ambition and Imagination, which are above all properties of Adolescence.

And one thing more.

There was Innocence and Innocence.

There was an aloof, transcendent purity, the innocence of a child, that continued, strengthened by knowledge, clear-eyed to old age.

Then there was another kind ; something active, born of trouble and defeat, of humour, sorrow and despair ; a Magdalene innocence ; and this because, to William, there was in repentance that initial innocence of childhood. A return to it.

And this he held firm.

Yes, and he even went so far as to say that Byron, that soiled Byron, was not without a little of this. Who is it that quoted of him :

" . . . *il a souffert ; c'était une autre innocence* ? "

Well, they were right.

But William could not stomach Byron. Took him for all in all a cross-eyed fool. Perverse. Getting no kick out of vice or virtue.

Vice and Virtue. Sin and Innocence ; unmodish words in a non-committal age. But it would pass.

William got up, stretching, and went into the hall to wind up the grandfather clock, with much clatter of weights and chains.

CHAPTER XVII

EARLY next morning Johnny lay awake staring at his dormitory ceiling. It was strangely white.

Then as he dozed, the creature in the next bed began to stir with yawns and snorts. Then, sitting up, he called out: " My God ! " and : " It's been snowing ! "

And so it had. No wonder the ceiling was so bright. Johnny, squatting on his heels, craned his neck and looked out upon the landscape—neat white fields, black hedges and a muddled opal-and-oyster sky, far away, with pale blue rifts.

It was not freezing ; there was no snow upon the trees.

That day was a Saint's Day, and at breakfast Fenn was asked to find out from William if there would be tobogganing.

William, in his study, was preoccupied, and answered at last that if they really wanted to go rolling in three inches of slush, he supposed they could.

At noon, one came asking for the key of the barn, for the House toboggans were kept there. These had been knocked together in the village in the colder winters of past years.

There were six in all; four of moderate size, and two monsters, with superb steel runners. Nigel and Gray and others in authority hauled them out from behind William's dumb piano in the barn. Cobwebs lay thick upon them.

Gray annexed one of the monsters " for us and our friends," and giving Johnny sandpaper, set him to work on the runners. As it was improbable that Johnny would get near any of the House toboggans, Gray lent him his old red tea-tray. After dinner William's House repaired to their private track, which ran steeply down a field parallel to the road to the village. The start of the run lay just beyond the junior football field, and William sitting in his study was disturbed all the afternoon by the shouting.

About half-past four John Fenn strolled across The Duds' Pitch and the football field over a wide path trampled in the slush. The wind was getting up, a mild wind which would thaw most of this in a night.

He came to the crest of the slope.

The sun was low in the sky. Below lay the village, parti-coloured where the snow had slid off the roofs. And about the village were the marshes, and flood-water golden in the sun.

Fenn joined the crowd.

The six House toboggans were doing heavy work, and there were besides some queer craft in use; flotsam and jetsam.

There was a huge slow-moving grocery crate, on wooden runners; a play-box half-way down the

course and stationary, its owners scared and marooned in the traffic.

And there was a bench upside down, resembling a canoe, furiously paddled with hockey-sticks.

Fenn saw Johnny setting off decorously, legs crossed, a neat dot, upon a red tray. And he saw Gray and Nigel there, as uproarious as upon Rat Day; and Nigel in the same old sun-bonnet.

They were surging about one of the larger to-boggans, manning it for a race, and shouting to another gang in charge of its rival, who were toiling up the coffee-coloured slope.

At length these reached the top, panting, and the two monsters were set side by side on the crest of the hill.

It was decided that the crews should sit this trip, instead of lying one boy on top of another. Fenn declined offers of a safe seat in the middle of either toboggan, but he said he would start them.

Penhurst was arranging the order.

" Gray, you come stroke if you please, and tuck your bandies well under you, mind ! "

Gray was pushed forward.

" Now who's got long legs here ? " continued Penhurst.

" Nigel, you go last, and lean right back parallel to the ground, and everyone hold on to his legs. Sit closer."

At last they were settled, and then began a frantic shouting to clear the course ; and all down the track there was a scattering to left and right.

Fenn started them : " Are you ready—go ! "

They went.

The two eager boys holding on at the rear of the toboggans let go with a shove and a kick ; but one crew had not set their head quite straight, and in righting this, lost ground, giving Penhurst and company a lead of several yards, which they increased, keeping the centre of the track.

" Fore ! " they howled, though there was no one in the way.

" Lean back ! Lean back ! God ! These bumps ! "

" I can't. I'm slipping off. Hold my legs, dam' you, hold my legs ! " shrieked Nigel ; and then he was no longer seated upon wood, and the slush was penetrating. He made a desperate effort to haul himself back on to the toboggan. Jerking his legs, he kicked, so that they could hold him no longer. In an instant he slipped off behind, rolling in the snow, searing his face. There was a yell from the oncoming crew, all violently braking with their feet ; but he was under them—one runner struck him, before, slithering sideways, the toboggan overturned. . . .

Polly, Miss Greig, was plumping up her bright cushions after a tea-party.

Her guests, spinsters, not of this parish, departed after an early tea to catch their train.

Mrs. Dean, the weather being what it was, lent the car, and Kedge to drive it down to the station.

And how the dear things had talked, and gossiped too ! And Polly had let them run on to their hearts' content. For, after all, the proper study of mankind *is* man, and that did seem to excuse gossip to a very great extent.

It was now only ten past four and very light in her sitting-room, because of the time of year, and because of the snow.

Miss Greig opened the window just a crack. What weather for the apple trees ! And fancy Mr. Dean giving leave for tobogganing in this ! If she had known in time, she would have told him how impossible it was to dry all those clothes. As it was, the drying-rooms were only just sufficient for all the shorts and sweaters that came in after the cross-country runs. But to go and countenance tobogganing when it wasn't even freezing ! It was too thoughtless of Mr. Dean. But then Mr. Dean was a thoughtless man. He just didn't think. That was what was wrong with him. She returned to the fire, a nice little blaze, and began sorting out songs for the evening, when Julia would play for her, and one of the music masters was to bring his fiddle, and one of Mr. Warner's boys his 'cello ; so there would be trios too.

Last time there was music she had discussed intervals with Bentley major ; and he had said that a ' second ' in music had for him all the sharp sweetness of an acidulated drop.

But she was not sure he wasn't having a little joke when he said that !

Kneeling, she separated the songs, making two piles upon her verdant carpet.

And in her room, as William said, it was not the busy wallpaper that jarred, nor the Alma-Tademas upon it ; but rather their union with the furniture, which was angular and painted in triangles and spots.   And there was a bowl of tooth-powder pink hyacinths, and a shelf of guide-books of the " So You're Going to Jericho " series.

Then Polly heard footsteps, and there was a knocking on the door.

William came in.   He spoke quietly :

" Will you come, please ; there's been an accident.   Nigel Bentley has been crushed, tobogganing.   They've taken him straight up to the Sickroom.   I didn't get there until they were half-way up the top stairs.   I only wish they'd come for you straight away."

And when the school doctor came he said Nigel could not be moved to the Sick-house.

Half an hour later Kedge, returning from the village, was sent straight back again to send a telegram ; whilst William started on a trunk-call.   Now William had taken up telephoning late in life, and embroiled himself with the Exchange.

The wind was rising, and it rose all that evening.

Late in the afternoon of the following day they operated with difficulty in the Sick-room of William's House.   Dimly Nigel felt himself lifted on to a table.   He knew how he was lying : straight out as upon a tombstone.

Somewhere there was a great pain, and he was bound up with it.

He came a little nearer to the movement about him ; and there were voices.

Daylight coloured his eyelids a warm dun. Then something came about his face, and there was a smell, oncoming, invading. Now it was a taste too ; cloying, damnably sweet. He fought it, and made a desperate effort to put his thoughts in order, and tell himself where and who he was.

He clenched his hands. They seemed a million miles away. He gasped, taking larger breaths. He belonged to the smell now ; it was his element. His teeth felt as large as dice ; but he was getting rid of his body ; then dull pins and needles came, and slowly he turned head over-heels into space. . . .

That evening the wind reached gale-force. Lavender sat by the fire in William's dining-room and listened to its booming.

Julia was there, and John Fenn ; while Mark waited up in the Sick-room with William, until Nigel should come round.

In the dining-room no one spoke. Lavender stared into the heart of the fire. Tim slept on the floor, his legs in a bunch.

Presently a maid came in to draw the curtains, and a boy to summon Fenn to Preparation ; for there were no bells.

John Fenn knocked out his pipe and got up to go.

Julia spoke to Lavender: "Would you like
Johnny to come and sit with you?" she asked.

"I wouldn't, if I were you," said Fenn. "Let
him keep his mind on his work now, and I'll send
him along later to say good night."

"Yes," said Julia. "And he shall have supper
with you upstairs."

John Fenn put his pipe away in his pocket.
"Would you like a book or anything?" he asked.

Lavender shook her head.

"I'm going to play a little," said Julia, and she
moved over to the spinet.

"Good night, Lavender," and John Fenn closed
the door.

*   *   *   *   *

"You do wrong to take me out o' the grave;
. . . I am bound upon a wheel of fire. . . ."

Nigel was coming round.

Opposite his bed was a fire-place with spear-
shaped leaves upon the tiles surrounding it. These
curled upon their stems, and intertwined intolerably
before his eyes. They wavered and grew. He
must disentangle them, and know what they
were. Explain them. But he couldn't, and
they drew his eyes and wove their pattern on
his brain.

If only he could lie down flat; he could explain
them then. But his head and shoulders were so
high; and then below came a great burning,

lashed to him, strapping him down ; and those leaves went on waving and curling. . . .

In a little while he knew he was at school. But then, how could he be, when he heard his father's voice ? In a weary anger he toiled with the idea, and left it unexplained.

The minutes went by heavily.

There was a spout to his lips, and something wet in his mouth, remote. It didn't reach his palate or his tongue. He knew what it looked like —water trickling into dust, faintly coated, but unmixed with it.

They gave him morphia at one o'clock ; but morning came in the same tangled agony.

The wind blew all day with a whip-lash of rain, and the snow melted.

The wind, tearing the mists, showed the bending trees, gaunt and storm-tossed ; and by evening there was nothing but patches of snow, left shrivelled and smutty beneath the hedges.

At the end of the day came hail, lashing the windows. The noise was intolerable, and the stones came down the chimney, spitting into the fire.

Nigel stirred. So that was hail. And then his mind cleared suddenly, and he opened his eyes.

There was movement at the window. Kedge was up a ladder outside.

Nigel knew him and saw him against a wild sky, his lank hair tossing in the wind. His face was puzzled and patient, as always ; and out there in the storm there was something about him of that sweet fool of Lear's. Under Miss Greig's guidance from within, he nailed up wads of sacking, shutting out the last of the daylight, and the crack of the hailstones was smothered.

That night Nigel slept again heavily, with morphia; and soon after midnight he woke.

Polly was there with grapes, peeled and stoned, to take away the taste in his mouth.

The storm howled incessantly. Polly went behind a screen by the fire and drank tea with the night-nurse.

There came a stronger buffet of wind, striking the house. "The poor sailors at sea!" she exclaimed. But coming from her that meant nothing. She said it if a twig stirred!

Nigel dozed again, and the only thing he knew was the voice of the wind; it accompanied him. He drifted further into sleep; and it seemed that he was at a great and dizzy height, and as though the wind moaned about a lighthouse, and a dark sea lashed the rocks below. It grew taller and taller, swaying—and he fell from it, leaving his inside at the top.

He woke again, drenched with sweat, grasping the sheet; and there was Polly with new pyjamas, dry and warm.

Towards morning he slept again, and it was Lord's Schools *v.* the Rest, upon a great white plain, and he was lost for ever, finding the Rest; and the glare scorched his eyes; but the plain shrivelled and became, with unspeakable relief, the white of the nursery tablecloth; and they took breakfast together in the garden, at home, in the sun.

* * * * *

And William talked with Lavender.

She came to say good-bye to him three days later. William said there was no hurry ; so she stayed talking to him while Mark had his last few words with the school doctor. And they spoke of what Nigel would do when fit again ; and of what Johnny would do in the future ; and then William asked after her own plans.

Lavender told him of Paris to come, and 'cello lessons, and of how she hoped to start again right from the beginning, and what her music master said of her smattery work.

" Um," said William. " And are you mad on this 'cello, or is it just a drawing-room accomplishment ? "

" Oh, I love it ; but I've not enough finish for the drawing-room, nor the grit or patience to go further."

" But you're going to start again."

" Yes, perhaps."

" And what else do you love ? Do you write ? "

" Oh, no, I could never write."

" How do you know ? Nigel has it in him ; and Johnny is bursting with something too."

" Yes, isn't he ! I think it's going to be Drama."

But William thought it would be world politics.

" And you," he continued, " do you read much ? "

" Yes. I think I do. But that's not enough ; I must have active self-expression."

At the word ' self-expression ' William drew in
his mouth as if eating a sloe.

" My good child," he said, " if you have any
grit or genius it will out. Otherwise the desire
for what you call ' self-expression ' is a brand of
vanity-cum-laziness ; a short cut to notoriety without hard work, and an inability to perceive that
you may be nothing out of the ordinary after all."

Lavender's chin went up, not in indignation, but
interest. Her eyes shone. " I know," she said,
" and I've sometimes understood that. But you
know, when you read poetry, especially the
Romantics, and get a glimpse of what they're after,
the whole complexion of life changes, and you feel
you must express yourself."

And she went on about the Romantic poets and
the ' Star ' they followed, far off in a luminous
mist ; the revelation of Truth in Beauty.

William sat with shoulders hunched, and compared her with her brothers.

Emotional and communicative she was. And
William said again : " My good child, the point
is not, I think, that we should strive, one and all,
to express ourselves in paint, wood, words, stone,
clay, raffia, or any other medium.

" The point is for us to have seen the ' Star,'
as you call it, even if we can't follow it ; for then
we have part and lot with poetry, even though we
go no further than talking of the weather, arranging the flowers, and picking out the National
Anthem with one finger.

" But you are not ungifted," William said.

"Maybe in time you'll express yourself. But that depends on whether you have grit enough to accept your limitations, and then go on working, tooth and nail."

And she must remember that although she might have her head in the clouds, in company with Shelley and others, the result of this communion, if she tried to reproduce it, would probably be inferior ; but if sincere, quite printable. If that happened she must be content ; and in contentment go on trying harder than ever.

"And one thing more," said William ; "they tell me that a good actor takes pleasure in playing a small part to perfection ; and that is the way to look at insignificant lives."

Lavender pushed back her hair and laughed, and told William he was a tonic.

Then out he came with his usual : "Things are never as bad as they seem, except when they're worse."

*   *   *   *   *

"... and hark the crowing cock, how drowsily it crew."

Nigel had never been so wide awake.

It was ten days since William spoke to Lavender, and two in the morning.

Nigel had not slept since the "Lights Out" bell had roused him.

The firelight blinked on the ceiling, and now and then a coal fell.

233

The gales had passed, and the silence sang loud in his ears.

He lay with one leg bent, and the pillows pulled down about his ears. His mind was clear at last. Earlier in the evening he had said to Polly: " I shall be fit for cricket next term, shan't I ? "

" Cricket next term ! " The good lady was astonished. " You mustn't think of next term," she said. " What you've got to do is to get fit for Oxford."

" But, good Lord, that's six months ahead ! "

" And you'll well need the time to recover in, after an operation such as you've had."

And with a certain relish she told him how his crushed inside had been straightened out. Nigel, listening with one ear, caught the word spleen, and said he'd met the word in Literature ; and put the idea of six months' inactivity out of his mind.

But that was hours ago. He listened to the fire, going flicker and plop. And the hands of the clock went round. Polly's carriage clock tick-ticked on the silence, intruding upon him.

To it he said : " How, is, my, lit, tle, friend ? " Inquiring for some time. But Dombey's ploy grew wearisome, so he said instead :

> " How odd
> Of God
> To choose
> The Jews."

—his favourite poem, and it went well to the ticking of Polly's carriage clock.

Every quarter of the hour came the chime from the Chapel Tower, measurely.

And then the cocks began to crow, clear, and from great distances, faint, drawn-out, linking up the farms.

The sky was violet. At four, Polly brought him tea, weak and fragrant; and sipping, he watched the sky change.

At six there were sounds about the House, of servants, and a cart went by, down the hill. The early bell at seven ended his vigil, and in the rising clatter he began to sleep; a sleep that ' slid into his soul.'

PART III

MIDSUMMER

CHAPTER XVIII

" Your actions are my dreams."
—" *A Winter's Tale.*"

ONE day in May Gray finished writing to Nigel,
and rolled over on to his back.

It was a pearly day; and the sun, half hidden,
warm upon his eyelids. He lay out on the cricket
field against William's garden wall; and high
above, the lime leaves unfolded, pale and crinkled.

And there were voices and the dull, echoing thud
of someone beating a study carpet. This stopped
in time, and Gray rolled over again on to his front.
Close to his nose the grass smelt sweet, and somewhere a lark mounted thrilling, into the haze.
Gray lay with inturned toes and an empty mind.

On the far side of the field they were rolling; a
clanking hum and the plodding of a horse. . . .

The following day Nigel got his letter by second
post, and read it in the garden after tea. He was
alone. Mark had been called out to the coast;
some fisherman had thrown a fit amongst his lobster
pots. And Lavender was in Paris.

Nigel lay in a long chair. He was still bandaged
round the middle and shaky upon his legs.

On a milking-stool beside him was a pile of books

239

and papers, and upon him a rug and yet more books.

Over the lawn the swallows wheeled and dipped, and beyond, the kitchen gardens sloped down to the orchard and the river.

Nigel inserted his thumb and tore open Gray's letter. He was impatient for news, for William's barn had been burnt down, and there were pictures of the ruin in yesterday's papers.

" My good Boy " (he read)—" Such goings on ! Have you seen the pictures in the papers ? It *was* a blaze, and all in the middle of the night, too. They haven't an idea how it started. They just got the cars out in time, (Fenn has one this term.) But all William's jumble. every stick of it, was burnt to ashes.

" The first I knew of it was Penhurst pounding on my face ; the alarum ringing ; a scuffle of feet on the boards, and a hellish red gloom and crackling outside.

" We shut all the windows, Pen and I, and then slithered downstairs. Everywhere was drenched. The fools had cantered down with the fire buckets at enormous speed and spilt gallons.

" When we reached the courtyard, the entire House were there, leaping about in *négligé*, and half of them with bare feet as well ; and William in a tartan dressing-gown directing that hose of his he has for the car. About as much use as a penny squirt.

" And everyone was there, just everyone. I do wish you had seen the woman Turvey moaning in a shawl. Poor old gargoyle, there was some excuse for thinking the Trump had sounded ! I told her twice myself, that it hadn't, and then someone led her back into the house.

" Actually there wasn't very much we could do. The fire engine was on the way up from the village. William's hose was quite useless ; so short and no power. Besides, the fire was getting hold of the back of the barn. All he could do was to souse the doors and the front wall and a bit of the eaves. Luckily what wind there was was dead away from the House. But there were splinters flying, and the air was bitter and full of blacks, and trembling up above the roof. And birds and bats and rats and all the things that lived there were coming out.

" I never thought flames could get up to that height with such a roar. It was seen for miles right away down the valley. There's not been such a blaze since Waterloo !

" And then the flames began creeping out under the side-eaves with wispy smoke ; sort of supple they were. Rather beastly ; and the smoke was going away from us into the trees in clouds. They were badly scorched. This morning I went down there, and on the Barn side all the leaves were brown and frizzled ; queer sight, just as if we'd leapt into Autumn.

" All the extinguishers were used up at once, so we collected the empty buckets and made a chain from William's lily pond in the rose-garden. Fenn and I filled the buckets, and as the water was low I stepped in, so as to fill them quicker. It was about knee-deep and damned cold. I got tangled in the lily roots, and the slime at the bottom surged up between my toes. And then I trod on what felt like a bundle of knives and cut my foot. This morning we dragged the pond and fished up a plaguey tin pleasure boat belonging to William's brats. One of Papa's Xmas gifts, sunk years ago in his ornamental water, and rusty. It will probably end in my having my foot off. Housemasters' children !

"Well, I stood there pushing down buckets on to the lily leaves, everyone telling me to hurry up. It was almost dark there behind the yews, and cold after the heat in the courtyard; we could hear the rest of them shouting; and then there was more glare and crackle, and a most frightful roar and collapse, as the bulk of the roof fell in.

"Soon after that we heard the engine creaking on the hill; and got to the yard just as it swept in through the gates. It was not as smart a turn-out as I had hoped. I thought to see brass and bells, burnished helmets and vermilion paint. But what came in through the gates was a dray and a hand-pump, and a job-lot of old friends sitting round it, legs a-dangle. They might have been going to market! Still, we cheered them and hauled the younger boys out of their way.

"Several old friends, as I said; the grocer's lad—you know, the one with curls and a hare-lip; and Mr. Wallah, who always throws an extra nut into my bag after the scales have turned; and that fellow from the garage with the frog legs, my double; and the man from the wine-shop; and both Publicans, bless them! I gave Hind-and-Panther a hand down from the engine myself, all dazed and unshaven in his uniform.

"Well, they didn't even look at the barn to start with; they soused the near side of the House in case the wind changed, and gave the dormitory windows a fine wash down. But directly the Pompiers arrived William started sending everyone back to bed, very crisply; all except us prefects.

"He saw me wringing his ornamental water out of my pyjamas, and sent me up to change. Now my dormitory was all right, because Pen and I shut all the windows

before we came down ; but below us the floors were awash,
and most of the beds soaked too, and the walls opposite
the windows all streaky and tear-stained. Those gallant
fellows must have trained the hoses straight in through
the windows. I really never realised how near one is to
death by drowning in a fire ! Really it was stranger in
there than outside, with the lights on, and all those little
swine paddling about in it, enjoying themselves, so beastly
wide awake, and sitting on their soggy beds pulling splinters
out of their repulsive red feet, and Polly going to and fro,
distract in a kimono, calling to heaven that every boy
would catch his death of cold.

" Actually, everyone was as warm as toast, and panting.
We'd been on the go ever since the alarm rang ; and that
was only half an hour ago, though it seemed six months.
It was then about 1.30. I stayed up there and helped
Polly for a bit. We sent them to the Changing rooms for
sponges, and got the worst off the floor, squeezing them
out of the windows on to the heads of William and the
prefects.

" Yes, and I caught your John standing plumb in the
middle of the gangway, squelching up and down upon
his sponge in a dream ! Then Polly went off down to
the kitchens to boil milk ; and Johnny and I went round
turning mattresses and collecting damp bedding. Finally
these pampered wretches were made comfortable with
other peoples' rugs and dressing-gowns, and the ward was
in order by the time Polly arrived with the milk. She even
tried to press a glass on me.

" Then William looked in and thanked them all for
helping ; and they kept saying : ' Not at all, Sir, we enjoyed it.' The fools. As if they'd been picking his apples
for him, or playing ring-a-ring-of-roses with his children.

And the poor man did look done. I suppose he thought the House might have caught at any time; and I think he must have been very fond of that barn.

" I went down with him again to the courtyard. The House was pretty quiet by that time, and the Pompiers were packing up.

" They had got the fire under almost at once. The barn, or what you could see of it now the flames had gone down, was just a huge charred shell; but the whole length of front wall and the doors were intact. And there were new arrivals with torches, gaping at it all. The man Warner, very spruce, in a polo coat, asking for information. I can tell you he made me feel shabby; me in me old brown and buff jacket, and the legs of the slumber-wear I bought in your county Town when I stayed with you. I wonder what you would have worn, dear, if you'd been there? Your old sun-bonnet, I expect.

" Besides Warner I saw Kettle, making a personal reconnaissance of the ruins.

" And Kedge was there now, fully dressed and hatted. The master would take it to heart, he said. Then I ran into the School-house porter, just going home to stop the Proprietor from coming down himself to identify the dead. Apparently everyone thought it was the House itself which had been gutted; and the Houses were turning out to help, when Mrs. Dean sent round to say it was only the Barn. They tell me Teacher had trouble getting his lot back to bed again, and lulling them off to sleep.

" When everyone had gone away we went up and had tea with William in his study. Polly and Mrs. had left it all ready. We stood about drinking in complete silence. Quite flat and tired we all were of a sudden. It felt like the end of an unsuccessful party, when you're only too thankful to finish up the scraps and go to bed.

" The morning after it was given out at breakfast (a foul breakfast with no milk, Polly having given it all to those little swine the night before) that there was an extra ' half ' for us to sleep it all off. And all through the day the clearing up went on. Servants came from other Houses to help put ours to rights ; and mattresses were out airing on William's lawn.

" The extinguisher man came too, and by evening we were ship-shape and trim for another fire, if heaven willed it.

" Pen and I inspected the ruins. Inside the shell there was a wide circle where the cars had been ; and then a mash of broken and blackened tiles, charred wood and ashes. We rootled about and found wheels, just the rims, and spokes, all twisted out by the heat ; and the entrails of William's dumb piano, I should guess ; and the runners of that toboggan that stove in your ribs, cockled and still warm in the ashes. That's about all."

And here the letter ended.

Four days later Nigel got another.

" My last letter," wrote Gray, " was an extra, to tell you about the fire. This is an ordinary one, and I hope you're going on well. Johnny says you loll in the garden, eating peaches and pancreas.

" And even here it's tranquil. I think the pace of things slows down in the summer term. And this is no exception. There is a lot of the usual sitting about in the sun.

" William is now in full wrangle with the Insurance Company. He thinks he knows how the fire started. You know all that cockled iron that Pen and I had a look at the morning after ? Well, Fenn and Kettle went through it again with William who explained every piece. The wheels we found were all that remained of two prams and a Bath chair ; and right in the corner where the fire started was something that William identified as an old tin trunk. One of those mustard-coloured abominations. It had been turned into a hay-box so that the woman Turvey could make the porridge over night ; only that was stopped because it tasted musty. We complained about it in a body. Well, it seems that Kedge and the underlings removed the trunk to the Barn with the hay still in it ; and Kedge remembers that the lid was half open. Now Fenn the scientist comes forward saying that if by any chance the hay was damp, an intense heat would have resulted from its confinement in the trunk ; enough to set the hay on fire ; and hence the destruction of William's ¡unk and Barn.

" I don't think much of that. I know it happens with stacks if the hay is damp and taken up too early ; but this hay was last year's, I believe ; and as the trunk was kept in the kitchen, in which I am told the heat is perennially equatorial, there is every reason to suppose, as I told Fenn, that this hay was bone-dry when removed to the Barn. And the young man is none too pleased at the explosion of his theories. But I don't see what it matters, anyway. The place was burnt out, but the front wall is apparently sound, perfectly sound ; and there are plans afoot to build a couple more fives courts behind it, using it ; there is room on either side of the doors. This won't affect us, though. It's a pity it couldn't have happened in our time. A separate garage is to be built alongside the fives courts.

" The courtyard is in a terrible state. To-day a gang arrived to take away the wreckage and sort bricks. Slow, bovine men, with red handkerchiefs and string below the knee. I went into your study to have a look at them before dinner.

" They were encamped against the Barn doors ; bread and cheese going and bottles of cold tea tilted against their lips, and they had those royal-blue enamel cans with lids to them. Why do they always have those, and what's in them, anyway ?

" Kedge was there, telling them to make themselves at home, I suppose, when suddenly that old hag flounced out upon them from the kitchen, and gave them one of her verbal trouncings.

" I couldn't hear what she said, but it broke them up, and the last I saw of Turvey was her back view, elbows working, penguin-feet at 90°, flapping back into the kitchen.

" Have you ever noticed her hair-pins ? They're like croquet hoops."

And Gray gave other news : (William's children had played hockey out on the field with a woolly ball and father's canes. Penhurst had a growling appendix, and was off bowling and beating and golf.)

" But he walked round the links last night with William and Teacher and enjoyed it. They got in among the trees, and William was stung by nettles, and Teacher said how *Providential* it was that dock-leaves grew near nettles ; and William said : ' Not at all. Not at all. They like the same soil.' Oh, and did I tell you that Polly Minor is dead ? Kedge is very much upset ; but William is giving him a canary. I met Kedge brooding on the cinder path, last night after nets ; and he told me what Mrs. Turvey said about his rhubarb. On and on he went, and there I stood upon the cinder path, all sympathy ; the shadows growing longer on the field, and Kedge joining the end of each sentence on to the beginning of the next. Good night."

Nigel put away the letter in a book, where Lavender found it five years later.

Gray wrote every week, and so did William, sending or recommending books.

In his first letter he had said :

" It is sharp for you missing your last term and a possible place in the XI. But you should count it nothing but a blessing that your long years of busy idleness here should have ended suddenly in this brief period of calm. Sort your thoughts, and go up to Oxford with a clear head."

And Nigel lived all day in the garden, and slept there. He read most of the day, and often far into the night ; so that moths, ichneumon flies and daddy-longlegs came out of the darkness and seethed about his lamp in the summer-house. Each day he walked a little farther ; up and down the paths in the vegetable garden. And it was ten years since he had known a vegetable garden in early summer ; for at his Prep. school there had been nothing but turf and the sea in the distance ; and at William's house more turf running up to the walls of his kitchen gardens, which were out of bounds.

And now the sight of this early promise and pale uniform greenness took him back to the times when he had come here before breakfast to eat peas young and sweet in the pod, and the garden walls were as high as cliffs.

And then of a morning, after a drink of milk, he would saunter out with Lavender to take off the eschscholtzias' hats for them, and tie up bumble-bees in the canterbury bells. And so those " pot-hook and hanger " days had given place to summer terms at school, when, as Gray said, the pace of things slowed down ; and there had been, year after year, that sitting about in the sun, especially after a shower when the turf smelt and the leaves glistened, and William would come shooting through his door in the wall and out on to the field to cry :

" Get up off that grass ! "

And the passion of House matches, and School matches, when you took your rug and lay amongst a cluster of companions, obscure and secure ; some-where on the immense circle of spectators ; and you there, biting grass and passing remarks upon members of the XI, white and holy, standing out there in the glare. And the Chapel bell chimed the quarters of the hour.

And ordinary days, the periods of unpalatable work, followed by nets after tea, and so to bed by daylight.

Then the bathing ; the splashing and hoarse

voices magnified; the water's glitter, its movement, its greenness and its taste. The feel of wet
matting on the spring-boards; and Kettle's diving
instruction. For in summer Kettle came into
prominence. He seemed to swell, especially on
Field Days, thriving on the pomp and dust and
sweat of these affairs. And the Inspection, too,
for which he toiled, abusive of the officers of the
O.T.C., yet furious if they took any of his work
away. And what with getting the Eight off to
Bisley and preparing for Camp—well, as he said, he
never shut an eye the summer through !

And those preparations for Camp. By half-
term Kettle was head-over-ears in them. The eve
of a Crusade must have been tranquil in comparison.

And the Band. How he nourished it !

Last year the Corps were returning from a Route
March through the village and up the hill, with the
Band in full blast, when from William's tradesmen's
entrance out comes Mrs. Turvey, thinking to have
heard the 'Salivation' Army.

And Kettle said if there was any more tomfoolery
about the Band it should not go to Camp.

Then an Old Boy gave four silver bugles; and
the Band played all its tunes every evening on the
Parade Ground.

William put wool in his ears and said : " Heaven
preserve me from Brass Wind ! "

* * * * *

And now William's phrases belonged to a past
life—a life retreating into memory and reminiscence.

For such an age had passed since that sunset when Nigel had kicked the slush from his feet and climbed on to the back of a toboggan, that his existence in William's House was as remote and clear as childhood. He was divided from it by pain and loneliness—by silence and by thought.

So he lived in the garden, reading and detached ; his tongue still in his head for hours at a time ; and this to him was singular after years of chatter ; but he returned to William's House in every letter he received from it. And each morning he woke early, when the earth was grey with dew ; and overhead came birds, wheeling slowly, bright under wing in the sun. So he woke early, partly because he was out of doors, and partly because it was in his family to do so. Mark did ; Johnny did ; and so also Lavender ; and so in time her son, Nigel John Fenn, who, one May morning ten years later, pushed his bright head against the netting over his cot and said :

" Not mornin' yet ? With the birds singin' and the sun shinin' ! What a thing to tell a child ! "

CHAPTER XIX

" . . . The fayre sunshine in somers day.
That when a dreadfull storme away is flit,
Thrugh the broad world doth spred his goodly way
At sight whereof each bird that sits on spray,
And every beast that to his den was fled
Comes forth afresh out of their late dismay
And to the light lift up theyr drouping hed."
—SPENSER.

THE season of flies had come again, and Gray
brought out his bamboo pole with the wineglass lashed to its head.

To-day, in June, the air was heavy and a-buzz
with the creatures, in that Johnny found no small
difficulty in trapping them ; so active were they in
their prime.

And little wonder that they were alert, seeing
that it was the early afternoon ; no time for fly-
catching. For Gray had laid down that this be
done in the evening when the creatures were drowsy
upon his ceiling ; but he was away chatting with
Kettle in the armoury, and Johnny, who was low
that day, had, to cheer himself, invited Clitheroe
to come in and lend a hand with the bamboo
pole.

It was 1.30. In a few minutes Clitheroe would be going away to change into flannels, for it was a half-holiday. But Johnny was due at two o'clock in William's classroom to juggle with x's and y's; having after many months exhausted William's patience.

So the pole came out, and the wineglass, and the methylated spirit from a bottle; the same that had served in the autumn.

With a lot of chat and explanation the pole was raised on high, mauve fluid tipping and swaying; flies curving easily away in all directions.

Johnny caught nothing.

Then Clitheroe took his turn. Eagerly he grasped the pole, and to have more reach, half climbed upon Gray's table. And seeing three flies struggling together angrily, he swooped up at them and caught them on the wing. In a flash they were imprisoned against the ceiling, and after a moment dropped buzzing into the wineglass overcome by fumes.

Then Clitheroe in his pride grew reckless. He swooped at single flies who were not preoccupied with quarrelling, and the methylated spirit slopped over the brim.

Johnny stood below, encouraging.

Now during all this chase, Gray was returning from the armoury. He reached the House and came into his study just as Clitheroe lost his balance and clattered down, spilling dead flies and spirit all over Johnny's head and the table—coming to rest at Gray's feet amongst the shivers of the wineglass.

Gray, in rising fury, gave no time for explana-
tions, nor asked what Clitheroe, a stranger and
no fag of his, was doing in his study.   Straightway
he pushed aside his table and beat them both, so
that the dust rose ; and casting them out into the
passage, he recovered his temper almost as soon as
it settled again.

But in the corridor they gasped, and Clitheroe,
to show that he could speak, managed to say :
" My God, how that stuff stinks !   You'll have
to wash your head."

Johnny had no time and the aroma lingered
in his hair ; so that as he walked up the
road to William's classroom, the air, clammy
against his scalp, was saturate with methylated
spirit.

And sorely he sat down to do an algebra paper
for William in which there was little he knew and
a great deal he had no wish to know.   Frog was
there, reading, at the other end of the room ;   there
to enforce this work, for William had been called in
to help decide the last place in the XI.

After a long, barren pause, Johnny laid down
his pen.

Clovis-Abel looked up.   " What is it ? " he asked.
" This work, it goes not ? "

" It hasn't started," said Johnny.

In all good nature Clovis-Abel stepped down from
the daïs to have a look at it.

Now William's paper was concerned with alge-
braical multiplication ; all bound up with the
question of plus and minus, it was, as Johnny

knew ; but the signs went wrong, invariably, inevitably.

" But here," said Frog, " there is no difficulty."

" But no," Johnny agreed, " none ; if one but understood."

Clovis-Abel sat down at a desk alongside him ; and bending over him, sniffed.

" What is it," he asked, " that you have in the hair ?   You are a fag.   You are not allowed to oil the hair ?   It seems to me that it is alcohol ; how do you call it ?   Spirit ? "

" Yes," said Johnny, pink with indignation, " it's spirit.   Mucky methylated spirit spilt over me in an accident, and I've washed my head and it's getting stronger and stronger !   I can hardly breathe."

" It is worse for me, sitting over you."

Johnny expressed concern, and knotting his handkerchief at the four corners, put it on his head.

" And now this work."   On a clean sheet of paper, Clovis-Abel wrote down William's first question.   " Listen to me," he said ; " forget the numbers and think only of the signs.   You shall call *plus* ' my friend,' and *minus* ' mine enemy.' And everything shall be clear."

And behold it was so.

For when Johnny came to multiply *plus this* by *minus that*, he translated under the Frog's guidance, saying :

" The friend of my enemy is my enemy."

Secondly, when William asked what $-15p \times -7q$

was equal to, they brushed aside these p's and q's, and chanted slowly together :

" The enemy of mine enemy is my friend."

And then they worked out fifteen times seven. Johnny was entranced.

Clovis-Abel smiled. " One could work it out with real friends and enemies," he said.

But Johnny thought not. Considering, he turned his greenish eyes on Clovis-Abel.

" It only works in theory," he said.

And Clovis-Abel reluctantly agreed. It was, indeed, only in theory that your friend was your friend's friend.

However, this immaculate theory of friendship carried them through the remainder of William's sums.

At the end Johnny thanked the Frog very warmly, and in his gratitude stayed chatting, his handkerchief still knotted on his head.

He told him he was going to keep the ' friend and enemy ' plan to himself, and because of it Algebra would never be quite so repulsive to him again.

Clovis-Abel was pleased.

" Soon," he said, " when you shall know a little more of mathematics and a little more of my language, you shall find this useful in the future for your geometry " ; and he wrote a rhyme upon a scrap of paper :

" Le carré de l'hypotenuse
Est égal, si je ne m'abuse,
A la somme des deux carrés
Construits sur les autres côtés."

Johnny read it through. What was it about? he asked. And Clovis-Abel said a certain sort of triangle. Johnny nodded. Perhaps it could be added to the triangles in his Confidential General Knowledge Paper; and folded Frog's rhyme and stowed it away in an inner pocket with his precious Hebrew Roll of questions. Then they got up to go, and Johnny left his work upon William's desk. Walking stiffly, he left Frog with a smile.

The smell of methylated spirit was by now less pungent in his hair.

Clovis-Abel went down to the fields to find William somewhere in the tangle of nets beyond Big Side. The sky was sullen; and from the east, ragged copper clouds were coming up.

The sun shone hot and dull; and then was hidden, so that an oppressive shade passed over the turf.

On the silence came the knock-knocking of balls at the nets; dull or sharp, echoing in the trees. Clovis-Abel approached these cricketers with some caution, knowing not when and where he might be hit.

As he came up, William detached himself from a group round one of the nets.

" And did that little wretch get through the work I set him? "

" Yes indeed." And Clovis-Abel hoped that William would not mind his having helped Bentley with an explanation.

William answered that he didn't mind who helped the child if its outlook could in any way be cleared.

257   R

" He looks at all the things I teach him from the wrong angle ; and I keep him in from time to time, because he mustn't be allowed to think that he's a special case. I'm going up to Common Room for half an hour."

" So am I," said Frog.

" You come home to tea with me afterwards ? "

" Please," said Clovis-Abel.

Later they walked down the road to William's House, and on either side the trees stood heavy and silent. The birds, too, were quiet. William looked up at the sky and said they were in for a storm.

Clovis-Abel agreed, looking down at his dusty shoes.

At last they reached the dining room.

The french windows opened wide on to the lawn ; and there was Julia, pale and cool in her Puritan frock—grey, with deep white muslin collar and cuffs.

She had started tea, as had Miss Greig, who in a dizzy gingham gesticulated towards a bowl in the centre of the table.

" Strawberries, Mr. Dean ! " she cried, " and such beautiful berries ! "

" Not out of my garden ? " asked William.

" Oh, dear me, no. Mrs. Throssell sent them round ; some of her early ones, grown under glass."

And William said that it was very kind of Mrs. Throssell ; but that they must divide his share between them. Picked strawberries of any kind were wasted upon him ; what he liked was to crawl under the net and eat them hot in the sun. " And I don't think they should be in that bowl," he added.

That bowl, usually filled with flowers, was of green glass, and valuable ; an old Milk Bowl, shallow, with a hollow rim, into which earwigs crept and ran round and round till they died. . . .

John Fenn, in flannels, came in with the afternoon post.

There were bills and circulars for William and Julia, and a letter for Miss Greig from the brother in Mexico, with all the latest oil-gossip.

John Fenn had heard from his mother in Paris. He asked leave to read it.

" Do," said William, drinking tea and rustling among his circulars. Julia talked with Clovis-Abel. Towards the end of her letter Mrs. Fenn said she had seen Lavender.

" Yesterday," she wrote, " the chameleon child came to see me, and stayed to tea. I see very little of Mark in her ; but she answers your description : long throat, grey eyes and slim hands.

" Well, and what am I to say about her ? You were quite right, she *is* affected. Pretty phrases come too easily to her. Her charm is exhausting. She talked and talked about the school, the masters, you, her brothers and that accident last term. I'm glad the brother is going on all right. Then she told me about her French family here, and her 'cello lessons.

" She seemed happy. You said she changes with whoever she happens to be with. You know, John, she can't help playing a part, I think. I don't believe she has a real Self except in times of great happiness or perhaps disaster. But then on those occasions it's not hard to be sincere. Well, John, she's young and aggravating and purposeless, and I love her, and next Sunday we are going to Fontainebleau together."

That was the end of the letter. John Fenn put it away, and with a pounding heart began to squash his strawberries.

Juice spurted upon the white cloth.

" Naughty ! " said William, pointing at the stain ; and Miss Greig rose up to insert a saucer and pour boiling water upon it. " And if you do it again, you'll go straight up to bed," concluded William with severity, passing the cream. Then he changed the subject. " Taunton," he said, " is going to get that last place in the XI."

Fenn agreed.

Taunton was captain of Throssell's House, who on Rat Day was hung head-downwards over the pigsty.

" Apart from his batting, his ground-fielding is the best I've seen in recent years. Better than Nigel Bentley's. If *he*'d been here, though, he might have got in. I always said he was a good bat."

Miss Greig, coming out of her Mexican news, caught the word " back," as she thought ; and aware that the conversation turned upon Nigel Bentley, said she'd always understood that he played wing three-quarter.

Amid laughter, her thoughts were brought up to date But William did not even smile.

" Now, Mr. Dean," said Polly merrily, " I shan't mind your laughing at me ! " For she prided herself on being able to join in a laugh against herself.

But William shook his head and sighed. She must pardon him, he said ; he very seldom laughed at all now. Very seldom.

But surely there were still some things that roused his humour ?

Oh, yes. William thought there were certainly one or two things. Poodles for instance, and Recitative, and the Chairman of the Governors. And he sent up his cup for more tea, with an air of bringing the question to an end.

" William," said Julia, " it's just a year ago to-day since you went up to London ! "

There was general laughter, in which Clovis-Abel joined immoderately, repeating : " Ah, the visit to London ! "

Fenn laughed also, having heard the tale from Clovis-Abel.

William lowered his head into his hands.

" Do not tease me," he said.

As for this day a year ago, he classed it with certain others in his life—black patches—as when in November he had run over the dead pig.

It all arose out of Throssell's finances. For Teacher, a nervous breadwinner, had for some time past been going upon the hypothesis that all lawyers, in company with stockbrokers and accountants, were not only knaves but fools, and he had dispensed with them in favour of a little book called ' Every Man His Own Solicitor.' And upon his affairs becoming greatly entangled, he had been forced by his wife, that shrewd lady, to return to his late advisers, and to make several personal and costly appointments. And Mrs. Throssell had supplemented these in advance, by sharp letters all round, commanding that no unnecessary expense be incurred ; and each adviser had written back saying this should be observed, charging six-and-eightpence a letter.

Now Teacher had confided in William, who had suggested that they should make the best of a bad business, and taking advantage of the sunny weather and a half-holiday, go up together in his car for these expensive interviews ; rounding off the day with a little opera at Covent Garden, and a drive home by moonlight, arriving at dawn, D.V.

And the Proprietor had been so nice about the whole thing ; and they had managed the journey up—William driving in his hat with the generous brim—and they had managed the traffic and the interviews, and then had darted into a hastily-chosen restaurant to eat and drink before the Opera.

William started off with soup—thick soup. And now I will tell you what he found at the bottom of his plate, having drunk it all : a hair-pin !

Now after that meal they had separated, to meet again shortly at Covent Garden.

But William, parking his car illicitly, went into a Pharmacie for lozenges, and came out of it at speed to join his friend. Springing into his car, he was about to drive away, when a dark-blue shadow loomed beside him, saying : " Wait a moment,

sir." In shock and surprise, William jumped,
letting in the clutch with a bang.

The vehicle sprang forward—as did the officer,
clutching a door-handle.

It was then that William was taken for a car-
thief; and in a fluster of irritation was unable
to furnish correctly the number of his own car.

And to top it all, his licence was far away, deep
in the poacher-pocket of his winter overcoat.

Oh, and it had been a weary business of expostula-
tion and reply! Finally, with the officer bulging
beside him, William drove off to Covent Garden,
that Teacher might identify him.

Then, sadly jangled, he was assuaged by the
richness of the Opera.

Yes. They *had* driven home by moonlight; and
their final breakdown came at cockcrow, at the
bottom of the hill; so that Kedge was roused in
his cottage, and came out to help them in his night-
shirt.

" That day!" said William, "full of memories;
and all for nothing, since they tell me he's reverted
to ' Every Man His Own Solicitor.'"

" My good William," said Julia slowly, "who is
it that tells you these things? Be more explicit."

But all William could tell her was that he felt it
in his bones. "And it's going to rain," he said;
" we shan't get our tennis."

He had arranged a four that evening with John
Fenn, Warner and Throssell.

Fenn's game was above the average; Warner's,
too, was worth watching.

So was Teacher's; he pranced forward between his first and second faults; a gambit which lent both style and incident to a game devoid of skill. As for William, he liked to serve with old, dark-brown balls, quite soft, that shot away at wizard angles over the clover.

But now they heard a rumbling overhead.

William held up his finger: "Is that thunder? or are they making beds?"

Beds! At four in the afternoon! That was what he always said; as though bed-making was an irregular event, brought to the ears from time to time like thunder, or the intermittent sounds of rock-blasting down the valley!

But this was thunder, muttering overhead and all round the horizon.

The air was dry and dark and waiting.

Fenn's terrier came quietly in from the garden and subsided on the mat, his head upon his paws. Then came a wind, restless in the trees; and the first of the rain, a few huge drops, dark as old pennies on the paving-stones outside.

A pause; then lightning, and thunder all on top of it—a splintering crack; and the full force of the rain.

Down it came—a curtain between them and the trees; striking hard upon the leaves and turf; so that Mary Greig sprang up and flew out of the room and away to make sure that all small junior boys were safe indoors. John Fenn went too, less hastily, and Timmy at his heels with drooping tail.

And as he went, he heard from the direction of

the boys' wing, the scream of dormitory windows, thrown up and shut against the rain.

But William and Julia and Clovis-Abel stood together in the dining room, watching the storm. And to them came the smell of grass and plants, reviving ; and of rain falling on hot earth ; a midsummer smell, catching in their throats. . . .

After a while the sky lightened ; yet there was heavier rain. The light grew in a changing sky ; the turf began to shine and the leaves in William's flower beds were brilliant, dripping upon black earth.

And William watched the rain, falling lightly now, an airy curtain between him and the darkness of the trees.

Then through the door in the wall came Kedge, squelching over the lawn towards them, his clothing dark with rain.

He brought bad news.

Caught in the potting-shed by the storm, and fair deafened by the rain upon a tin roof, he had grown uneasy, thinking of Madam's Orpingtons ; and when the worst was over, had made down the garden to the orchard, only to find the bulk of them dead and warm ; crushed in the mouth of their house, in the stampede for shelter when the storm first burst.

Kedge was greatly upset.

First the barn had gone and got ablaze ; then his poor parrot was taken ; and now two score Orpingtons, fine lusty birds, struck down in a storm !

He made no doubt that they'd panicked into one house, silly-like !

He supposed the young gentlemen could eat them for dinner.

" No, I won't have that," said Julia.

William perpended, while the rain dripped off Kedge's chin.

Clovis-Abel made a suggestion. " Could we not," he said, " take the dead fowls to a poulterer, who might buy them, as they have only just died ? "

" Ah," said William, " that might be just worth while trying. Only it must be done directly. Kedge, you go and fetch them, and I'll get the car out. We'll take them straight down to Jenkinson's."

Kedge touched his forehead and made off.

" Kedge ! Kedge ! " Julia called after him in sudden alarm, " are the turkeys all right ? "

Kedge hurried back. Turkeys ? Yes, Madam ; safe and sound, sound and safe. He'd left them strutting proud in the orchard, and the light shining blood-red through their wattles ; blood-red it were, blood-red.

William waved him away.

" Julia, I'll take those corpses down to the village."

" Oh, no, my love ; you know nothing of fowls or bargaining. It's not in your line. I'll take Kedge."

" Well, he'd best change his clothes first. He's as wet as a sponge."

" Oh, no, I can't wait for that. He might have to go to bed till they were dry, or appear in his Sunday ones. No. I'll go alone."

Clovis-Abel offered to accompany her ; but Julia,
thanking him, shook her head, and smiling good-
bye, went out into the courtyard with William.
They passed by the kitchen windows, blurred by
the heat within, and sudden fall of temperature
without, and down to a disused coal-house, beyond
the nursery wing, where the car had been kept since
the barn disaster.

William squeezed in, avoiding the walls, white-
washed, but dim with coal-dust.

" William, shall we get any insurance for those
birds ? "

" Not a penny." In gloom, William was convinced
of it.

" Act of God," he said, " that's the line they'll
take, you'll see, especially after all this Barn business." And he was about to express himself on
Insurance Companies, when Kedge arrived with
the Orpingtons in a laundry-hamper.

Julia drove away down the hill.

And poured over the valley was a greenish light,
strange and brilliant ; and to the North the storm
clouds, gigantic, purple, moved away. The wet
country-side was shining in this light ; the roofs
and windows caught it in the village. Julia slipped
down between the hedges ; the tyres sounding
' swish ' upon the roads criss-crossed by rivulets;
and the ditch where William had once left the Pig
gurgled with running water.

On the outskirts of the village she saw a man
walking towards her with great strides. It was
Warner, who for once had miscalculated Nature's

mood, and had been caught without shelter upon those wide open spaces beyond the marshes.

And now he was striding home as briskly as his clinging wet clothes would allow. As the car drew level, he raised a pulped Panama.

Julia commiserated with him and told him briefly of the Orpington disaster.

Loud in sympathy, Warner urged her to drive on to Jenkinson's. But when he heard her story, Mr. Jenkinson the poulterer shook his head.

There could be no eating market, he said, for poor fowls who'd died in hot blood and fear. No sale for them mangled and crushed.

And he fetched a clean sheet of newspaper and spread it over the dead birds.

" You never ought, Ma'am," he concluded, " to 'ave 'ad all them fowls in one enclosure. If you'd a'ad them separated, this wouldn't a' happened. They'd 'a' got in at their own doors without harm, however panicky they'd a' been."

So Julia drove away, and picking up Warner on the hill, took him back to his house.

Then she returned to William, who was not surprised; but he sat down and wrote at length to the Insurance Company.

It was cold after the rain; and in the quiet the thrushes sang.

Kedge buried the Orpingtons.

Later, William sauntered out upon the field to view a sunset in bird's-egg blue and eau-de-nil.

CHAPTER XX

" I was for that time lifted above earth."

THE gardener and the gardener's boy got out the sailing-punt between them, and gave Nigel a push-off. Slowly the punt moved downstream with a following wind ; slowly, parting the water without sound ; and the grasses on the bank went by, one by one.

In mid-stream Nigel slackened his sheet—out it went, rattling through the blocks ; and he drew away from the boat-house.

It was early and the breeze scarce up ; and drawing away he looked back at the house, standing high above the orchard and the kitchen gardens.

Away to the right along the ridge were the tips of pine trees.

And the house looked westward, so that in the evening its windows shone for miles over a land of windmills ; a wide prospect of marshes, grey-green, and Norman towers ; a land of faint flowers and gently-moving sails.

In the afternoon he took the car and drove three miles down to the bridge—that limit of the perambulator walk. And all along the road the cow-parsley was stiff and fresh in the ditches.

As in the autumn, returning from that bathe, he stopped the car on the crown of the bridge, and looked down for some time into the water.

Then he drove the car into a field, and walking slowly, climbed up into a beech wood above. In the heart of it he sat down on last year's leaves, his back against a tree. Taking out a brand-new pipe and a pouch of golden tobacco, he found he had no matches, and put everything away again.

He leant back against the tree.

All around were beech trunks, shapely and snake-grey, rising slenderly with arched roots from the floor of the wood.

Under his fingers the moss was close, and he felt beech-nuts, sharp edges and shrunken sides.

There was a coolth in the wood, and a freshness left by rains ; and birds sang in its green shade. Far above the sun struck upon upper branches, and the leaves there shone transparently.

Then it was a cloud passed across his glimpse of the sky ; a white cloud so high and blazing. It took him back to a day in the autumn, a brilliant day of wind, when Gray had howled insults at those Colts, filling the air with his cries ; and watching the cloud he knew the vigour of that day again.

And it was one with the vigour that rose in him at the moment—surging up, a sense of confidence and power and great possessions.

And as he looked up through the leaves, this feeling grew. This confidence was not in himself but in the universe and beyond ; a shining certainty And so in the renaissance of his life—

knowing neither failure nor achievement, unpre-occupied by success—he shed his personality ; his power soared into an impersonality ; and in this freedom he had part and lot with an eternal loveliness.

In that moment there was no time ; and sin and death were irrelevant.

Nor was this a sudden miracle; but a fulfilment of something he had always known. A seed dormant in him ; stirring at times ; as when in childhood he had felt suddenly glad, with no accounting for it ; capering in a shining excite-ment before a nurse who said he would be crying before bedtime. And so he was, invariably.

And he had come near this present feeling a term ago, one spring evening in his study. Nor was that the first time. For he had known that sense of power most strongly, three years ago in Normandy ; bathing on a cold September evening, after rain.

He had swum far out, and, turning, saw the sky all torn and pale in the west, and the great sweep of the bay with one dark rider galloping across the sands.

And once again, at the end of a chain of thought, just staring at the ceiling of a railway carriage.

And now, high above through the leaves, the tip of the cloud still blazed ; and he looked down, and his eyes were blind in the shade of the wood.

CHAPTER XXI

"Il n'y a plus de printemps dans mon cœur."
—BAUDELAIRE.

So he came home, and on the tea-table there were letters for him.

Gray said :

"Did you have a monster thunder-storm about four last Saturday ? We did. It soused and it pelted and boomed overhead. The pitches haven't yet recovered from it. Most of William's poor wife's Orpingtons were suffocated in a stampede—trampled down in the mouth of their house ! And yet we didn't have boiled bird for supper that night, nor yet for dinner next day. So it's a dead loss for Mrs. D. unless William can get anything out of the Insurance."

Over the page he went on to tell of an incident down at the swimming-baths.

"Yesterday before tea at House-bathing," he said, "Fenn and I were chatting with our elbows on the lowest diving platform. There were legs swinging before us in a fringe, belonging to a crowd of undistinguished cricketers with no ' eye ' to be put out by bathing. They sat on the platform above. The afternoon sun was warm, and Fenn was asking me how your inside was getting on. I had just come out of the water, and he was just going in.

" Having carefully set the scene, I will now describe to you the apparition—the unbelievable creature—the veritable *cauchemar*—that bolted out of one of the masters' bathing-boxes and fell into the deep end.

" It was that man Frog, naked to the waist, and then came a pair of the most mirth-provoking zebra slips—black-and-white-stripe bathing-drawers—*caleçons*—how can I render them in words ?

" Well, he fell in and swam right down to the shallows and back again like a drowning dog. Hair plastered over the face ! If a porpoise had been flung in amongst us there could have been no more amazement. People scattered in the water, gasping ; and in the boxes dressing and undressing ceased. Then he hauled himself out and lay panting on the brink, like something washed up out of the seas.

" I laughed so much afterwards I had to have my braces done up for me. The suddenness of it all. No one knew the man was come down to the baths at all. And why at that time and with us ?

" The affair had a sequel, for while Frog was dressing some knave went and wrote : ' *Défense de se savonner* ' upon a paper, and pinned it to his door. Fenn caught sight of it and started inquiries. I sent for your John and asked him whether he had done it ; having seen him down there with companions. It was rather in his line, I thought, remembering Teacher's alcoholic troubles.

" But he swore no, and I'd only just sent him away when William sent for *me*, if you please. Although he did not suspect me of having written it, he would like to make certain I was taking no unorthodox steps to clear up the matter! Really, William does try me pretty hard at times!

" Still, as in a few weeks I shall be severing myself from him and his for ever, I shall probably overlook the way he has stung me verbally and otherwise ever since I came under his roof.

" And now for the National Game. The first round of the Colts started yesterday. We played Warner's. There was a lot of wanton overthrowing, but they got us all out for 102. Your John made 7 towards the Tail. The ball glanced off alternate hips till he was caught in the slips off his thumb.

" I must stop. Take care of yourself. They tell me you're coming down for the House-Supper. Then you can as usual eat side by side with me."

' Nothing will ever stop him talking,' thought Nigel. ' When his letters come it's as though he's chatting in the next room with the door ajar.' And he wondered if he himself were facetious, because Gray was ; or whether they had both picked it up from William all these years. But there was nothing like facetiousness for privacy. In all that cackle, who was to see your thoughts ? And phlegm and silence were foreign to their natures.

Johnny wrote in a large hand slanting over the page :

" Lavender has written," he said, " she sends her love. She's been to Fontainebleau with Fenn's mother. Fenn says he's going to take you sailing with him in September if you're fit enough. Has he written to you ? And could I have Timmy at home while you're away ?

" Yesterday Clitheroe and I went in to tea with Fenn. We had it up in his study, thank goodness ; I shouldn't relish feeding with William in the dining room.

" After tea I brushed Timmy down by the lily pond. I think he harbours fleas. He sits scratching his neck in an extasy and his collar revolved so that you keep seeing the name-plate.

" He's got a bottle of medecine now ; black treacle-stuff that smells. When he has it Fenn smothers his legs in a rug, and then you just slip a spoonful into his cheek ; and he gulps and runs away sneezing, with his head down. He lolls among the daisies on the bank and trundles himself scratching first one side of him, and then he turns and does the other. Last Sunday Fenn took him down the village and the Salvation Army Band was out playing and singing in a ring ; and Timmy went and sat down in the middle howling, and Fenn had to push in and pick him out. Yesterday poor Frog made a sight of himself down at the baths in nothing but striped shorts. Why does that look more naked than nothing on at all ? Some- one wrote ' *défense de se savonner* ' on his door. Gray thought it was me. I shouldn't dream of it. Frog's given me a tip for William's Algebra. Tell Pa I made a mouldy 7 against Warner's yesterday. We shall get them out for about 70 this afternoon. They're a stringy lot and Clitheroe will shatter them. He steps so high when he runs, and we shall all bank in close to fray their nerves. I wish I'd made more yesterday, but one day I'll get into double figures.

' Love

' from

" JOHNNY."

Nigel put both letters on the mantelpiece, and the cook came in. She was taking the servants down the garden to pick fruit. Would he make his own tea ? The kettle was on. And would he listen out for the telephone ? The doctor was away on the coast.

Nigel said he would.

The cook was a good party ; but inclined to be toothless until noon.

The third letter came from William. Nigel thrust in a knife to open it.

It was a brief letter. The man spoke again of careers ; but he spoke with a difference :

" I have pestered you overmuch to make a choice. As long as you're alert, I see no harm in delaying your decision for a year or two. I think you should write ; but don't rely on that alone. Remember, ' splendid speculation ' is not enough. It should have its counterpart of action. And I pray you when you write to snap your fingers at those like Zola and certain of our contemporaries, multiplying in these scurvy times—who go and reduce Life to its L.C.M. ; for they are in sensual blinkers.

" It's good that you are coming down for the House supper. Will you sleep in my house or in dormitory ? Either can be managed.

" Remember in future there is always room for you if you want to come down at the end of the Oxford Term, before we break up.

" If my house is full I shall bed you out at the King's Arms,' and you can run up the hill for your breakfast !

" Johnny seems doing well this term. I speak of his

cricket. Like you, he shapes as a fieldsman. Yesterday he got a few unsteady runs against Warner's young ones.

"I must stop. Kedge—that meek-hearted man—is waiting for the post, and one of my children has fallen down and cut his knees."

And he signed himself :

> "Yours ever,
> "WILLIAM DEAN."

Throughout the house the clocks ticked, and summer murmured in the garden.

William's letter pierced a numbness in his heart ; a blank tiredness that had come on him since the moment in the beech wood.

What had happened this afternoon ?

He probed his mind, and tried to recapture his detachment. But it was gone, and by his analysis he lost it.

Fidgeting, he tried again to lay hold of that shining certainty. But it was not at his command. For transcendent it had come at those other times and in the wood, unforced ; answering the exultation of his spirit.

And now he saw himself, shrivelled in the mind ; like some dim adult, who seeing the skies are heavenly, strives at a union with their loveliness, pointing, exclaiming, commenting—when a child would run out, look up, breathe and belong.

The more clearly he thought, the further was this vision from him. It was gone as dew from the grass. The very early morning of his life was over. A bright promise in the skies was overcome by creeping greyness, the early closing of his vision.

For he was no genius. What he had known in snatches was the Genius of Youth ; a supremacy ; god-like in detachment ; impersonal ; a splendid arrogance. Now, neither the torment nor the ecstasy of genius would come on him again. The memory of it he would carry through his life. And there was comfort in his desolation. The sharpness of his loss testified the power and the glory of this thing which had left him for ever. And there at the boundary of Youth he paused. This was nothing to make a fuss about. Not a loss to advertise. This was no particular case, and he'd had warning.

He'd heard William speak of *Mundane Blinkers* more than once ; and another William said : *this mortal coil* ; and a third : *shades of the prison-house.* And if ' these sorry, pinching mists ' were indeed closing in upon him, then he gave thanks that he could recognise them.

Until this time he had looked up proudly, and that light had shone into his eyes ; but now in this moment life unfolded before him with all its striving and tangle of human relationships—long, full, absorbing, prosperous maybe, or sorrowful ; and in it he saw tokens of that which was now behind the clouds :

278

"Eyesight, space and liberty."
"Laughter and thought and friends."

That loveliness, not made with hands, eternal in the heavens, was manifest on earth.

And in the recognition of this harmony was peace, if no more exultation.

So he faced his loss and came to the end of this thinking, and went upstairs and forgot the kettle for his tea, which boiled dry; so that the cook, returning, was greeted by the reek of hot metal.

Up in the bathroom he assembled beakers and draining-trays to develop photographs; and closed the shutters from without; so the light lay across the floor in bars. He worked on until the rooks came home, winging across the sky to the elms beside the house; and their cry was hoarse and deliberate.

Out beyond the shutters the sun slanted across the hill-sides. Smoke rose into the air, and wheels revolved upon the roads.

At six o'clock the "Publics" opened.

At six o'clock the factories disgorged; and in William's House the bell rang for tea.

Johnny heard it, lying on the field, and watched a green-fly climb a blade of grass.

Timmy sprinted by him, chasing swallows.

In the kitchen Mrs. Turvey cried for Glory's Sake to bring the tea-urns.

In the Sick-room Polly said "Hark!" and

listened for the cuckoo: "'In June I change my tune.' What did the old song say?"

But William continued up in his study—toiling and seething, and ten shillings out in his accounts.

THE END

*Some recent Constable fiction,
with press opinions of
its quality, is listed
overleaf*

D. L. MURRAY'S GREAT SUCCESS

STARDUST
A Tale of the Circus

BY

D. L. MURRAY
Author of *The Bride Adorned*

GERALD GOULD (*The Observer*) : " Enough material in a few pages to have made a whole story for the ordinary novelist . . . All richly conceived, all idiosyncratic and forcible and convincing and strange . . . And the horses and elephants ! . . And the noise and movement and glare and danger ! "

Birmingham Post : " A real melodrama of the old school describing the whole machinery of a circus and circus life. Unlike the old melodrama, however, it is admirably written ; its author is both a practised dramatist and the master of a fine and sensitive style . . . *Stardust* is a masterpiece of its genre."

Yorkshire Post : " A long novel of circus life, as full of thrills and adventure as anyone could desire. It is gloriously satisfying . . . The author is to be congratulated on a fine book."

CONSTABLE & CO LTD LONDON W.C.2

THE FLEET HALL INHERITANCE

BY

RICHARD KEVERNE

Author of William Cook, Antique Dealer

CONSTABLE & CO LTD LONDON W.C.2

EVELYN PEMBER'S CHARMING NOVEL

SO WE'LL GO NO MORE

BY

EVELYN PEMBER

Author of *Coucou*

Time and Tide : " Here is a novel of such rare excellence that it is hard to sing its praises. None of the new words fit ; one is reduced at length to the old word, quality. Not that Mrs. Pember is ' period,' she is almost disturbingly modern, but she has that out-of-date attribute, technique. . . . Buy the book with your last borrowed seven and sixpence. It is much too friendly a volume for the library list."

A. DUFF COOPER (*Broadcasting*) : " A carefully painted miniature in which due attention is given to every detail. . . . The characters both of the older and the younger woman are exquisitely drawn. There are also two minor characters who are compellingly life-like."

The Tablet : " This fresh and fine book is first-hand work. Nearly all the persons of the tale are creations, not replicas of familiar figures in the waxworks of conventional storytellers. Those of this book give us new hope for the English novel."

CONSTABLE & CO LTD LONDON W.C.2

THOMAS BURKE'S LIMEHOUSE TALES

THE PLEASANTRIES OF
OLD QUONG

BY

THOMAS BURKE

Author of *Limehouse Nights*

New Statesman : " Fifteen stories informed
with a hard vitality and an ancient and im-
placable wisdom, retold in a witty and beautiful prose which is yet essentially subordinated
to the unswerving progress of each narrative.
. . . Real story-telling."

GERALD GOULD (*Observer*) : " Mr. Burke is
to be congratulated on the restraint and force
of his new Limehouse tales. . . . He is a
story-teller, born and made. . . . All his gifts
are subdued to the one aim, the getting of
the maximum into and out of the story. Of
the sixteen items in his new volume, fifteen
open with a snap and go with a bang."

Bystander : " Humour, pathos, tragedy,
horror, you will find all four. . . . Each story
is a gem of narrative and characterisation in
its own way. A book not to be missed."

CONSTABLE & CO LTD LONDON W.C.2

ELIZABETH BOWEN'S LATEST NOVEL

FRIENDS AND RELATIONS

BY

ELIZABETH BOWEN

Author of *The Hotel*

Times Literary Supplement : " People who want all the ' i's ' dotted do not read Miss Elizabeth Bowen's darting novels with pleasure : those who can dart with her, even if they sometimes dart the wrong way in their anxiety to keep up, enjoy them immensely. *Friends and Relations* will not disappoint Miss Bowen's followers. . . . She is alternately Austenian and Meredithian, if one can use those terms as expressing the qualities modernized."

SYLVIA LYND in the *News-Chronicle :* " In *Friends and Relations* Miss Elizabeth Bowen has just stopped short of writing a masterpiece. . . . She has a singularly true sense of civilized life. . . . The four central characters move through a clearly-seen and brilliantly definite world. Miss Bowen never fails to keep our interest alert in them ; we are as alert at the end of the book as at the beginning. . . . A book really exceptionally rich in observation, wit and wisdom."

CONSTABLE & CO LTD LONDON W.C.2

VAL GIELGUD'S NOVEL of ADVENTURE

IMPERIAL TREASURE

BY

VAL GIELGUD

Author of *Black Gallantry*

FRANK SWINNERTON in the *Evening News* :
" A very excellent specimen of its kind. Mr.
Gielgud begins with secret service, a map, a
murder, departure for Poland, and an assault
in the train for Warsaw. . . . He does not
shrink from assassins, cracks on the head,
shootings, and similar violences. His book
moves at great speed and with great clearness.
It has inventive daring and superb confidence,
both geographical and historical. . . . The
best example of the ' yarn interesting but
steep ' that I have read for some years."

CLEMENCE DANE (*broadcasting*) : " A most
excellent story of the wildest intrigue, excite-
ment and adventure in four countries and
two continents . . . Not merely a thriller
. . . One of the best things of its kind since
Buchan's *Thirty-Nine Steps*."

Daily Express : " Mr. Gielgud can create
interest and suspense. He has produced not
only a ' thriller ' but a ' gripper.' "

CONSTABLE & CO LTD LONDON W.C.2

JOHN METCALFE'S MACABRE STORIES

JUDAS

and other Stories

BY

JOHN METCALFE

Author of *Arm's Length*

The Spectator: " Mr. Metcalfe, with his second book of short stories, sounds a note which may not be ignored. The individual quality of his work is hard to seize in words. . . .

Mr. Metcalfe, in Synge's phrase, shakes the fat of our hearts: he gets into even the most apparently humdrum interiors, and makes them uncomfortable. *Judas*, the title story, is thoroughly uncomfortable. *Funeral March of a Marionette* is more than uncomfortable. It is a small masterpiece in a key seldom heard among British writers . . .

" Those who are prepared for shocks, not to their susceptibilities but to their emotions, are advised not to miss *Judas*. They will find a writer who speaks always with his own voice and is, at his best, a master."

R. ELLIS ROBERTS in *The New Statesman:* " Beauty as well as terror is in these brilliant fantasies, that show Mr. Metcalfe as one of the greatest masters of the uncomfortable since Mr. Arthur Machen."

CONSTABLE & CO LTD LONDON W.C.2